Praise for
Jay Bennett's
previous suspense novels

THE DARK CORRIDOR

"Bennett has written another suspenseful novel, this time incorporating teenage suicide. . . . Will definitely appeal to mystery fans."

VOYA

THE HAUNTED ONE

"A poignant, gripping mystery which is hard to put down . . . Bennett is a master of psychological tension."

Midwest Book Review

THE SKELETON MAN

"Bennett weaves his story with a deft touch and a high level of suspense that will keep young adult readers turning the page."

Los Angeles Times

SING
ME A
DEATH
SONG

Jay Bennett

FAWCETT JUNIPER • NEW YORK

28527

A Fawcett Juniper Book
Published by Ballantine Books
Copyright © 1990 by Jay Bennett

Library of Congress Catalog Card Number: 89-24812

ISBN 0-449-70369-X

This edition published by arrangement with Franklin Watts, Inc.

Manufactured in the United States of America

First Ballantine Books Edition: January 1991

15 14 13 12 11 10 9 8 7

For Stan Bendetson
        Dear and Faithful Friend

Chapter

1

He dreamed.

And in his dream he saw his mother walking toward him, coming out of a night mist, walking slowly toward him. She had a black hood over her head, down to her shoulders, and he couldn't see her face. She wore a plain dress, very plain and severe. She held her arms close to her sides. Her hands were clenched. Clenched white in the darkness.

She walked slowly, very slowly, with measured steps, in a deep, dark silence. He thought he could see two vague forms at her sides, shadowing her as she walked. When she came close to him, she suddenly lifted the black hood, and he saw her white taut face.

And her eyes.

Her two large eyes.

"They are about to kill me, Jason."

"No," he whispered.

He reached out to her, but his hands touched emptiness

"Tonight."

Her voice was mournful and lost.

"They are finally killing me."

1

Her eyes were dark and glittering.

"Jason."

Her eyes were dark and pleading, pleading to his very soul for help.

"Jason."

"Mother," he whispered.

His white trembling hands were still reaching out to her, but they touched emptiness.

"Jason, please."

"Mother." That was all he could say.

"You have deserted me," she said.

"No."

"I called to you and you never came."

"That's not so," he said.

"Not even once." She shook her head, and her dark hair waved side to side. Her long dark hair.

"I'm alone. So desperately alone," she said.

"You wouldn't let me come visit you," he said. "Never."

But she didn't seem to hear or see him.

"Alone. Alone. Alone. Alone." Her voice, like a mournful chant, filled the air about him. "Alone. Alone. Alone."

She stopped suddenly, and the silence rushed in again, enveloping him.

For an instant she stood there staring at him. A hard, searing look. Her face became old, like a harsh mask.

He trembled.

Suddenly she turned her head away from him.

"They are coming for me," she said. "The footsteps are very near."

He tried to speak, but he couldn't.

"Don't you hear them?" she asked.

His lips opened, but no sound came.

"Save me, my son."

She had now turned back to him. Her face was now young and haunting, a lost, lost look in her dark eyes.

He heard footsteps on stone, soft and yet clattering.

"It's too late, Jason. They are here."

"Mother," he whispered.

"The executioners are here."

The footsteps had stopped, and all was silent.

Hollow and silent.

He heard her voice again. This time it was so quiet and sad he thought his heart would break.

"I've always loved you and you've failed me," she said.

"No."

"You're ashamed of me."

"That's not so."

"Then why are you letting me die, my son? Why?"

He couldn't speak.

She shook her head mournfully, and her dark hair waved, side to side. "It's no use. It's too late now."

"No, Mother. No."

"Good-bye, Jason."

And then he heard her say in a toneless voice, "Sing me a death song."

She drew away from his desperate hands, and the hood fell down upon her head.

The black hood.

Blotting out her face.

Her eyes.

He screamed and awoke.

Chapter

2

His Aunt Lydia was standing by his bed.

"You had a nightmare," she said.

"Yes, Lydia," he whispered.

"The same one?" she asked gently.

He nodded. "The same."

And he said to himself, You look so much like her. Just a bit taller, but the same deep brown eyes, the same dark, long, wavy hair. The same voice, low and modulated.

People used to say that you were twins. But you weren't.

Sisters. The Ross Sisters, who used to walk along broad Laurel Avenue, under the high royal palm trees. Walking side by side, faces glowing in the Florida sun. Hair iridescent. Matching each other, stride for stride, and talking lightly to each other.

Twins.

Alike.

So alike.

But oh, so different within.

You, Lydia, always quiet and controlled and successful.

And she, Marian, so . . . so impulsive. Very capable in

4

what she did but . . . impulsive. A desperately pretty but spoiled child. A child that never grew up.

Saw something she wanted and immediately reached out for it. Didn't care whom she hurt or destroyed.

An evil, spoiled child.

Isn't that what they still say about her?

Isn't it, Lydia?

Didn't the prosecutor use the very same words in his closing speech?

Shouting for punishment.

For death.

They all want to see her die.

The whole town is against her.

The town in which she was born.

Lydia, stop looking away from me.

That's my mother.

My mother they're killing.

Lydia.

He heard his aunt's voice come through the night mist.

The hall light was shining dimly behind her dark hair. Dark and black and glowing.

"You saw the item, Jason."

He nodded silently.

It was a news item tucked away in the back pages of *The New York Times*.

"The execution is set for next Friday."

"I know," he murmured.

"There is nothing we can do to stop it, Jason."

"Nothing?"

"Nothing."

"No," he said. "No."

Yet he knew that she had spent thousands of dollars of her money on legal fees and court costs. All through the eight long years since the first sentence of death was handed down.

Lydia had tried everything with a fierce, unrelenting persistence.

Even going to the governor as a last resort, taking Jason along with her.

5

But it was no use.

And now it was all coming to a final end.

Next Friday evening.

His eighteenth birthday.

On the day he was born, his mother was to die.

Lydia stood there, looking down on him.

"Your face is so pale," she said softly. "So very pale, Jason."

Outside, the night was silent and quiet.

Deathly quiet, he thought to himself bitterly.

Then he heard his aunt's low voice.

"You saw her again."

"I saw her," he said.

My mother, Lydia.

My only mother.

A fellow has but one mother.

He never has another one again.

Never in all eternity.

She stood there, her face white and drawn, as if she had heard every word he had said within to himself.

"Your mother," she said quietly.

She sat down on the bed and stroked his hair.

"Jason."

Her hand was cold, icy cold.

"It will soon be over, Jason. For you. For me. For Marian."

"It will never be over, Lydia," he said.

"I know. But nevertheless we must say it to ourselves."

He was silent.

"Until we get to believe it," she said.

He still didn't speak.

She bent over and kissed his cheek.

Her lips were cold.

"Try to sleep."

"I will, Lydia."

She stroked his hair tenderly.

"We'll go on, Jason. You and I. We'll go on."

"Yes," he said.

6

And then the two didn't speak anymore.

After a while she got up and went out of the room, leaving him alone.

Sing me a death song, Jason.

Chapter

3

He was ten years old then, and it was the last time he saw his mother. She was in a small, dusty room in the old prison, and he was alone with her.

There were some pale cigarette butts scattered over the gray stone floor. In the dull air, the stale smell of smoke.

He remembered that.

And he thought how his mother had always insisted on everything being clean and neat around her. In perfect order.

He breathed in and then kicked one of the butts into a corner and sat down.

A bare wooden table was between them.

The warden, who had grown up with Marian Feldon, even dated her, had ruled that there was to be no physical contact between mother and son.

A guard stood outside, looking in at them through a small glass window.

His face was hard and impassive. He had a scar on his right cheek. But his eyes were kind when they settled on Jason.

Jason remembered that.

And he remembered the words his mother said in a low, clear voice.

"You are going to live with Lydia in New York City. Over a thousand miles away from here. Where nobody will know who you are. She will give you her name. You are no longer Jason Feldon. You are Jason Ross. Do you understand?"

"No," he said.

"I don't want you paying for my crime," she said, her eyes hard and glittering.

The dark eyes that were always so tender with him.

"You didn't commit any crime," he said.

"How do you know?"

Her voice was harsh and bitter.

"I know," he said. "In my heart I know the truth."

"There is no truth. It's only what people say that counts. What they say in the court before a judge."

"You didn't commit any crime."

"The law says that I did. I'm a murderer."

He flinched as if she had slapped him.

And she had never touched him in anger in all his life.

"You didn't kill anybody," he said.

Never.

Even when he deserved punishment.

"The jury said that I did."

His voice was tight when he spoke again.

"But you told me that you didn't."

Her eyes flashed, and he could see the despair in them.

"Only you and Lydia and my lawyer believe me. No one else does."

He sat there looking across the pine table at her, at her white face with the dark eyes full upon him.

He wanted to weep, to reach out and hold her and comfort her.

But he did nothing.

"Jason," she said, and then was silent.

He got up and kicked away another butt and stood there.

He didn't sit down again.

9

He saw the eyes of the guard, and there was pain in them, and then he heard his mother's voice, flat and toneless.

"You'll live with Lydia. She'll be a good mother to you. Better than I've been. Much better. She loves you, Jason."

"I want to stay here," he said. "With you."

"You can't have me. The state has me now. Owns me. Body and soul."

He didn't speak.

"They won't let me go. They're going to kill me. Sooner or later. But they'll surely do it."

And then he heard her say, "Walk away from me. And never turn back."

"No."

"Lydia has nobody but you. She'll give you all her love."

"I want to stay and . . ." His voice trailed away into the stillness.

"And what?"

He didn't answer.

She spoke again, her voice low and harsh. "You'll do as I say."

"No. Never."

"Jason."

"Never," he almost shouted.

Then he turned away from her grim face and stared at the wall.

"Remember that, Jason. As I say."

Her right hand came down hard on the surface of the table. Making the whole table shake.

And he thought to himself with a sudden terror, You have fierce violence in you, Mother.

I never saw it in you before.

Was it always there?

Deep, deep within?

Hidden away from me?

And then the thought fled from him, and he sighed.

He stood rigid, looking at the blank wall.

A deep silence enveloped them.

He heard the distant sound of the *Silver Meteor* racing

10

along the tracks on its way to Miami, and he listened to the deep whistle, lone and chilling against a harsh sky, and he thought of the passengers sitting and talking and laughing on their smooth way to the sun coast.

He clenched his hands till the knuckles were white.

Then he heard her speak again, and this time her voice was soft and trembling. The harshness was gone out of it. He felt her heart speak in every word she said.

"Go, Jason. Please, Jason. Go, my son."

He bowed his head and put his fist to his mouth.

"Never come back. Never write to me."

The tears welled in his eyes.

"If you love me, as I know you do, you'll never come back to see me again."

He left without turning to look upon her face.

Chapter

4

All through the bleak years he never wrote a word to his mother. Nor she to him. He went to New York and lived with Lydia in her large East Side apartment.

He became Jason Ross.

Lydia, quietly and decisively, arranged everything.

She owned a successful real estate brokerage firm and introduced him to her staff as her adopted son.

Her sister's son.

She left it at that and explained nothing else.

She enrolled him at a prestigious private school as Jason Ross.

When he graduated from high school, Lydia was there with her influential friends, to see him get a top award.

She kissed him, and there were tears of joy and pride in her eyes.

And he held her close to him.

"Lydia."

"Jason, my son," she said.

And he let her say it.

It was the first time she had ever done it.

It warmed him. And eased the ache in his heart.

For underneath it all, he knew every moment of his life, every single moment, that his mother was at his side, aware of what he was thinking and doing, as if he had never walked away from her.

Never.

And she, Marian Feldon, was always with him.

He knew surely that one day the truth would come out and she would be set free.

He lived for that moment.

Until this last year, when he saw despair and defeat start to show in her lawyer's face.

"We're losing out, Lydia."

"No, Walter."

"Losing it all."

And Jason saw with a growing dread that the day would never come.

Everything was ending for her.

And for him.

All the hopes.

The illusions.

Next Friday at six o'clock in the evening, when day was fading away and the night was beginning to fall, Marian Feldon would be led from her cell.

Alone.

So alone.

"She will be put to death," he whispered.

My mother will be put to death.

And then, during the night, as he lay thinking of her and of the last time he had seen her, he heard again the sudden sound of the hand coming down hard on the wooden table. Like a thunderclap.

It pulled him upright in bed, and he began to shiver.

And as he did, the thought descended on him, enveloping him, and would give him no peace.

No rest.

Only terror.

Could she be guilty?

13

Could she?
Is Marian Feldon a murderer?
And am I the son of a murderer?
Am I?

Chapter

5

He stood in front of the gleaming skyscraper on the corner of Forty-seventh Street and Lexington Avenue. The sun flashed off his brown wavy hair, making it iridescent, like his mother's when she walked under a glowing Florida sky.

He went inside the building, walked through the crowded lobby and into one of the express elevators.

He had his mother's fine features, but he was much taller and well built.

One could easily see that he was Marian Feldon's son.

He did not have her dark, intense eyes.

His were gray.

Gray and quiet.

The elevator door opened, and he went down the corridor.

His breath held tight within him.

Chapter

6

He sat in the lawyer's office.

"There are only six days left," he said.

"I know, Jason,"

"Short days. Fast ones. They move too fast."

"They do."

"Isn't there anything more you can do?" Jason asked.

"Nothing."

"You've touched every base."

"Every single one."

"There must be something left," Jason said.

"There is nothing left."

The man, tall, balding, with neat, clean features, sat across the large leather-topped desk and gazed gently and patiently at Jason. He played with the lapel of his brown tweed jacket, his long, tapering thumb stroking the fine material.

You're a handsome, well-tailored, and fastidious man, Jason thought, and you're very dedicated and capable.

I've come to like you very much.

You've become almost like a father figure to me.

I never knew a father.

He died just before I was born.

And you have no children, Walter.

Walter Todman was a widower who lived alone in a Park Avenue condominium. He was an old friend of Lydia's.

She had persuaded him at the very beginning to take the case. And it was only because of him that Marian Feldon was still alive.

Jason knew that.

Todman broke the silence. "You didn't come here to speak about Friday, Jason."

"I know this is the end of the road," Jason said. "I know it too well."

"Then what are you here for?"

Jason looked at the man and hesitated.

"Tell me, Jason."

"The truth," Jason said. "I'm here for the truth."

Todman leaned toward him, his eyes alert. "What do you mean?"

"It's on my mind. And it's become unbearable."

He paused, and Todman waited.

Jason began to speak in a low, clear voice. "I've been rereading the newspaper accounts of years ago. Going over them again and again. They all say that my mother had a long affair with Arthur Madison. And then, when he wanted to leave her for another woman, she went to his office and killed him."

"And?"

"Late at night. No one else was there."

"Go on."

"She was standing over his body. The gun in her hand."

"That's how the police found her," Todman said.

"But she has always maintained her innocence. Says again and again that she didn't do it."

"I know that. Know it better than you. I've spent more

17

hours with her than anybody else. I know what she says, Jason.''

Todman lit a cigarette and then suddenly snuffed it out on the flat copper ashtray.

"Every word she says, Jason," he said softly.

He glanced down at the crushed cigarette and then back to the youth.

"Yes. You know," Jason murmured. Then he got up and went over to one of the wide windows and stood there looking out at the spire of the Chrysler Building, glistening like a pure-bladed spear in the noon sunshine.

All's well with this clean and shining world, he thought bitterly.

"Lydia has told me over and over how hard you fought for my mother. All of these long years," Jason said.

He paused and kept looking out the window.

His hands flat at his sides.

His face white and taut.

Todman sat there gazing at the back of the tall, silent figure.

"And, Jason?"

Jason spoke again. "You're considered one of the best trial lawyers in the country. You have a very impressive record."

"I've won some cases."

"But you're losing this one."

"I am," Todman said.

"It's hard to fool you, isn't it?"

"Maybe it is and maybe it isn't. Jason, what are you driving at?"

Jason turned and looked fully at the man. "I want you to tell me the truth."

"What truth?"

"Is my mother guilty?"

Todman paled. "I'm her lawyer," he said.

"And I'm her son. I want to know the truth."

"Why?"

"I have to live with myself. And with her."

Todman didn't speak.

"I'm not a kid of ten," Jason said. "I'm eighteen now. I want the truth."

"She has always maintained her innocence. You've already said that yourself."

"You're not answering me, Walter."

"Maybe I don't know the truth."

"You're still not answering me."

The phone rang, and Todman let it ring until it stopped.

"My secretary is out to lunch," he said. And then he said, "I have ten lawyers working for me, and nobody answers my phone."

But Jason's gray eyes were still on him, holding him.

"Walter," he said.

"She's guilty, Jason," Todman said.

"Guilty?"

Todman nodded slowly. "From the first day I took the case I knew she was guilty as charged. I've never changed my view."

"At no time?"

"At no time."

Jason bowed his head and closed his eyes.

"Regardless of what she said or still says, Jason. Guilty."

"No," Jason whispered.

"Yes. I've studied every bit of evidence over and over. Searching. Searching for one shred . . . one little shred which would . . . would. . . ."

He didn't finish.

Then Jason heard Todman's agonized voice shatter the silence. "Why did you open this up? Why?"

Jason didn't answer.

"It was better to leave it alone. So much better for everybody."

"I had to know," Jason said.

"Why?"

"I just had to."

Todman had risen from his seat, tall and tense.

"Why? Lydia lives with the illusion. Why couldn't you? We all have our illusions. If we don't, life becomes unbearable. Why did you set out to destroy this one, Jason? Why?"

Jason didn't speak.

There was a knock on the closed office door.

Todman turned sharply and shouted, "Later. Don't disturb me. Later."

His voice echoed out. . . .

A complete and vast stillness settled down over the two of them.

Heavy and impenetrable.

Jason felt that time had stopped.

Forever.

And as he turned away from Todman's pale, anguished face, he saw his mother's eyes, dark and sorrowful, full upon him, and he heard again her voice when she asked him to leave her forever.

Walk away, Jason, and never come back.

Because you are guilty, Mother?

Never see me again.

Guilty? Is that it, Mother?

Mother, Mother.

Then, as through a mist, he heard the man speak again. This time his voice was soft and pleading. "Jason, listen to me. Listen, son. I took the case out of pity."

"Pity?"

"Yes. I saw how the whole community had turned against her. Savagely. And she had done so much for it. She was an excellent school superintendent. Devoted and very capable. Known throughout the state. She could have gone elsewhere. To a much larger city."

He paused and went on.

"But she stayed there. Lydia had long before left for New York. Marian Feldon stayed home. And they all turned against her."

"She killed her lover," Jason said.

"Lovers have been killed before," Todman said fiercely. "This was a lynch mob. I was outraged. And then, with Lydia's persistence—begging to defend her innocent sister—I took the case."

"Knowing she was a murderer?"

"Knowing she was a murderer."

Jason turned abruptly away from the man and looked out the window again, and it seemed to him, in a blinding, terrifying instant, that there were spots of dark blood spattered over the gleaming spear of the Chrysler Building.

He put his hand defensively to his eyes, and the shimmering spots vanished as rapidly as they had come.

"I've come to care for Marian very much," Todman said.

"I know."

"To care for her in a deeply personal way. I'm a very lonely man these days, and I've come to look upon Marian . . . your mother . . ."

Jason turned away from the window and back to Todman, and he saw tears in the man's eyes.

"There is so much good in her, Jason," the man said.

"Nobody else says that."

"They're wrong. All wrong."

"They say it. They've written it. Article upon article," Jason said.

"Let them say it. Let them write it. But I've known her eight long years. They are all wrong. Every one of them."

He came closer to Jason.

"Keep your heart open for her," he said.

Jason was silent.

"She's alone. So desperately alone in this world."

Jason still didn't speak.

"I want to save her. With all my heart and soul. I've called upon everything I've ever learned in these many years in law. Everything."

His hands trembled.

"I want to save her. But I can't. I just can't."

21

Then he said in a low voice, "She's going to die."
The phone started ringing again.
Until it finally stopped.

Chapter

7

"Lovers have been killed before."
And you have killed yours.
And now what am I to do?
What, Mother?
What?
Shall I start hating you?
Your city hates you.
All your former friends.
Everybody.
For you have committed a most heinous crime.
That's how the prosecutor put it.
You have killed your lover.
In cold blood.
Killed him.
But your biggest crime in my eyes was your lying.
Letting me believe all this time that you were innocent.
Why?
Why did you do this to me?
"Why, Mother?"
He sat up and looked around him fearfully into the dark

night, and then he got out of bed and went over to a chair and sat down heavily.

Lydia came to the doorway and stood there looking at him.

He turned silently to her.

"Another dream, Jason?"

He shook his head. "No, Lydia. I haven't been sleeping."

"Just thinking?"

He nodded. "Yes."

And he wanted to ask Lydia, Do you know the truth? Did Walter Todman tell you the truth?

Or did you know it from the very beginning?

Did you, Lydia?

Did my mother tell you?

But there was so much anguish in her eyes that he didn't say anything. Anguish and guilt.

He wanted to say to her, It's not your fault that I can't sleep, Lydia. It really is not.

"Shall I stay with you, Jason?"

He shook his head. "Go back to bed," he said gently.

But she still stood there, gazing down on him, and he saw that something strange and new had come into her eyes. Something he just couldn't make out.

"Why are you looking at me that way, Jason?" She seemed to tremble just a bit.

He reached his hand out to hers and held it.

"It's nothing, Lydia," he said. "Nothing."

"I'll stay here with you. Just a little while, Jason."

"It would be of no use."

"Maybe it would."

"I'd rather be alone."

"Are you sure?" she asked.

"Yes."

And now he knew what the strange look was; a blend of fear had come into her deep suffering.

Quietly and subtly.

But it was there.

And it will stay there, Lydia.

For a long time to come.

Up to now she had been able to cover it with her superb self-control. But now it was breaking through to her inner core.

He still held her cold hand.

He pressed it tightly and then slowly let it go.

We are all going to break apart before this is over, he thought as he looked up into her pale face.

Her eyes met his.

"I love you very much, Jason," she said.

"I know, Lydia."

She bent over and kissed him on the forehead.

Her lips were cold.

Icy cold.

"Try to sleep, my son. Try."

"Yes, Lydia."

His heart went out to her.

"Sleep," she whispered.

Then he watched her leave, and he turned back to the window.

The night was vast and still, brooding over him like a great dark being.

Shall I hate you, Mother?

Shall I?

Chapter

8

He remembered lying on the beach under the Florida sun and looking up at the jeweled sky and then hearing his mother's voice. He turned to her. She had just come out of the water, and she was drying her hair with a beach towel. She laughed at him and began to sing in her low and melodious voice. Soon he was singing along with her. They finally stopped, quiet and content, just the two of them, alone on this stretch of beach, looking out to the sea.

Then her face began to pale, her eyes to get the sadness into them, and then he heard her say in a quiet voice:

"Sing me a death song, Jason."

He stared at her face, which was turned away from him, to the sea.

Once, when he was much younger, she told him that the Paiute Indians sang death songs, and as she had studied the Paiutes in a graduate course, she knew one of the songs. She sang it to him. He liked the sound of it, so she taught it to him, and after a while they sang it together.

Then, for no reason at all, they stopped singing it.

She turned back to him and smiled.

"Forget what I said."

"Sure."

"A wild thought. Like a passing cloud." She got up and shook her iridescent hair. "Let's go home."

"Okay."

But now he remembered in the darkness, for the first time in all the years, that it was on that night, that very night, that Arthur Madison was shot to death in his office.

It was a memory that he had buried.

Way, way down where he thought it would stay hidden forever.

But now it had come up.

And would no longer leave him.

Chapter

9

He was sitting with Carla on a bench overlooking the East River. They were on the Esplanade in Brooklyn Heights. Across from them was the skyline of Manhattan, clean and precise against a pure sky.

The sun sparkled off Carla's blond hair and fair face.

Her eyes were large and dark, almost like his mother's.

But his mother's eyes had bleak sadness in them.

Carla's were bright and alive.

They had been talking, and now they were silent.

He looked gently at her profile and thought.

Carla.

Carla Swenson.

Father Swedish and mother Mexican.

They had met and married in New York.

In this turbulent, dangerous, yet glowing city.

Why didn't my mother come here with Lydia years ago? Everything would have been so different.

Why didn't she?

"Carla, do you believe in fate?"

She shook her head. "No."

"Why not?" he asked.

"Because we make our own fate."

"What we do is what we become," he said.

"Yes."

"Your father?"

"What about my father?" Carla asked.

"Does he believe that, too?"

She smiled. "I don't know what he believes. He's a strange man."

"But you love him."

"Sure I love him," she said.

He hesitated and then spoke.

"Would you love him no matter what he did?"

She turned and looked steadily at him.

"You love somebody, you love somebody, Jason."

"Yes," he said in a low voice.

Her eyes softened. "My mother is strange, too. I have off-the-wall parents. But that's what makes life interesting, Jason."

"I guess so," he said.

"Life should always be interesting or it's not worth a crock. Isn't that so?"

"Yes," he said.

"Stop agreeing with me."

"Okay. I don't agree with you," he said.

"That's better."

They smiled at each other and were silent again.

Carla, he thought. I've known you for four years. We both went to the same school and graduated from it. I sat next to you in many classes. We went out together many times. I've kissed you many times. Said a lot of things to you. Things from the heart. Words I never said to anybody, not even to Lydia. And yet not once did I tell you that I was the son of a convicted murderer.

Not once.

Should I tell you now?

Should I take the chance?

It's become so hard to keep inside me.

So very hard.

Let me try.

Lydia is not my mother, Carla.

Carla, Carla, listen to me.

Yesterday afternoon I found out that my mother is guilty. She's a murderer.

And I'm the son of a murderer.

How am I to handle it?

I feel so bitter toward her now.

As if she had betrayed me.

Why didn't she tell me the truth?

Then I would find a reason to defend her.

Walter Todman knew the truth all the time, and he has fallen in love with her. I know that in his soul he has forgiven her. Has found reasons to justify her actions. But I . . . I, Carla . . .

I just don't know how to look on her now.

I just don't.

I feel so close to hatred that it terrifies me.

"Jason."

"Yes, Carla," he said quietly.

"There's a concert this Friday night. Van Halen."

"Friday?"

"I can get hold of some tickets. They're hard to come by."

"Friday?" he said again.

"Uh-huh. You doing something that night?"

"No."

"Would you like to go with me?" she asked.

He didn't answer.

"You sure your mother doesn't have something on?" Carla said.

"My mother?"

"She's always doing things."

"Yes," he said. "She's always going places."

"And most of the time taking you along with her. How about Friday?"

"She has nothing on that night," he said slowly.

He looked away from Carla, out across the gray river. He watched a freighter move slowly on its way to the Narrows.

Soon it will be out on the ocean he thought.

Out and away from everything

Just the sky and the sea.

Nothing else.

Away.

So far from everything that nothing can touch it anymore.

He heard her speak again. "Well, Jason?"

"That's five days from now," he said.

"I guess it is."

"Friday," he said again.

"Okay?"

He shrugged.

"Why not?" he murmured.

And then he turned away from her and gazed at the slow-moving freighter.

Chapter

10

She had once asked him why he called his mother Lydia.

"Why?"

"You do it all the time," Carla said.

"So?"

"It's a bit off center. Most people don't call their parents by their first names."

"I'm not interested in what most people do," he said quietly.

"Yes. I guess you're not, Jason."

Then he said, "I call her Lydia because it's the way things worked out."

He looked at her with his impenetrable gray eyes.

"Just leave it as it is, Carla."

She watched him walk off, tall and straight, and then the night took him away from her.

She sighed and went into her house.

Thinking of him.

And his mystery.

Chapter

11

He was standing at the railing of the terrace, looking out over the city as the sun set behind the tall buildings. Swiftly and savagely. Lydia had not yet come home from the office, and he was alone in the darkening apartment. He thought of Carla, of the slow-moving freighter seeking the open sea, and then he said to himself, There is no escape.

There never is.

One is caught in life.

Inevitably.

Soon my mother will be out of it all.

Released forever.

Free.

But I'll remain here, caught in the trap.

Caught.

Tortured.

Never escaping the pain, the hell, of memories.

Always seeing my mother with the black hood falling over her head and blotting out her dark, dark eyes.

"Mother," he whispered. "What have you done to me?"

His hand clenched into a fist. He felt his nails cutting into the flesh of his palm, and it was then that he heard the sound of the phone ringing.

"Lydia," he called.

And he remembered he was alone.

All alone.

He turned slowly and went across the terrace and into the shadowy living room and picked up the phone.

"Hello?"

"Jason Feldon?"

He stood there, not speaking.

It had been years since he had been called by that name.

"Is this Jason Felden?" the voice asked again.

It was a weak and whispery voice.

"Who are you?" Jason asked.

"Never mind that. I must see you."

"Why?"

"I'm in room 308. The Sloan-Kettering Hospital," the voice said.

Jason was silent.

The man spoke again. "I'm a cancer patient. With no time left. I must see you."

"Why?" Jason asked.

"It's about your mother."

"What?"

"Marian Feldon."

Jason felt a chill settle over him. "What about her?"

"Come now."

"I said, What about her?" Jason's voice echoed in the empty room.

"Room 308. Frank Morgan."

And then he heard the fading voice speak again. "Tell nobody. Come alone."

There was a click.

He stood there, gripping the phone and looking into his mother's dark eyes.

"Jason?"

He turned and saw Lydia standing in the shadow of the room; the key in her hand glistened.

He slowly set the receiver back onto its cradle.

"You look shaken, Jason. What is it?"

"It's nothing," he said.

"But . . ."

"Nothing," he said coldly.

She stood there silently looking at him, and he felt a great pity for her.

"I'm going out for a while, Lydia."

"Out?"

"Yes."

She came closer to him.

"But I thought we'd have dinner together," she said.

He shook his head. "I've changed my mind."

"But why, Jason?"

A sudden urge to tell her came upon him, but he heard himself say, "I don't know. Just changed it."

"Why?"

"Lydia, leave it alone. Will you?"

She came still closer to him and put her hand out and touched his gently, pleadingly. "Jason, we must try to help each other these days. We must."

"I know."

"These awful days and nights."

"I . . . I just want to be alone for a while," he said.

"Please stay home."

He shook his head. "I can't, Lydia. I have to go out by myself."

"But . . ."

"Just have to, Lydia."

"Jason," she murmured, her lips trembling. "Please stay here."

He shook his head. "Nothing I can do about it," he said.

And he left her standing there alone.

Her face was beginning to take on the bleak sadness of his mother's.

Chapter

12

As he stood on the dark street corner, under the cold lamp-light, waiting for the bus to take him across the park, he saw Walter Todman walking slowly down the long block. He was about to cross over to meet the lawyer and tell him all about the telephone call when the bus pulled up between them. Jason hesitated and then stepped inside, and as he did, he realized that he had made a life decision.

He was letting fate carry him along, wherever it wanted to.

The doors closed shut.

He looked out the window and watched the lawyer's lean and anxious face vanish into the night.

Chapter

13

He opened the door of the dim hospital room and saw a man sitting on a black leather chair, looking out at the night.

"Close it," the man said.

Jason shut the door and leaned against it, his shadow falling onto the floor.

Long and slanting.

"You told no one?" the man asked.

Jason silently nodded.

The man's face was narrow and haggard. It had a yellowish tinge to it. The skin of the cheeks was like parchment. His features were sharp and angular. He wore a thin light blue robe.

His head was bald.

He motioned with his lean hand to the bed.

"Sit."

"I'll stand," Jason said.

"Okay. Then stand."

The man sat there, now gazing directly at Jason. And Jason saw that the only strength remaining in him was in the eyes.

They were blue and steady.

The eyes of a young man looking grimly into death.

You're only in your forties, Jason thought, but you look old and wasted.

He felt an instant pity for the man.

"Get me a glass of water."

Jason filled a glass and then set it on the small table near the man.

"I'm Frank Morgan. The name mean anything to you?"

"No."

Jason had to lean forward to hear him.

The man's voice was low and weak but steady. Sometimes it dropped to a whisper, but it continued on, as if pushed forward by a grim will.

"I remember seeing you at the trial," Morgan said. "You were ten years old then. You came twice. And then you didn't come anymore."

"That's how my mother wanted it," Jason said.

"You're a good son."

"I'm a son. I don't know how good I am."

"A good son. I know it. In my bones I know it," Morgan said.

"Then you know it," Jason said coldly.

The man shrugged his shoulders wearily. "I have no children," he said. "My wife took them away from me. When we split up. They're with her all the time. They've come to hate me."

He paused, closed his eyes, rested, and then spoke again.

"You weren't in court the day I testified."

"Against my mother?" Jason asked.

"Yes."

He looked away from Jason's cold face and then picked up the glass and sipped the water. It dribbled a bit over his lips and onto his chin. He set the glass down again.

He put his frail hand to his naked head and let it rest there for a moment and then let it fall back hopelessly to his lap.

"They even took my hair away," he said as if to himself.

And he seemed to forget Jason and where he was.

"I had thick, wavy hair. And now it's gone. Gone."

He sat there, staring out at the black night that hung over the silent city.

Suddenly he spoke again. "When you're dying, they take everything away from you. Even your hair. These treatments make you bald. You know that, don't you?"

"Yes," Jason said.

"But they're no use. No use. You know that, too, don't you?"

Jason didn't answer him.

"You're going to die, you die. No stopping that, is there?"

There was a silence, and Jason felt like turning away from the man and walking out of the room. Slamming the door.

Then he heard.

"I was the chief detective on the case."

"You?"

"Captain Frank Morgan. The name should mean something to you now. Captain Morgan."

And Jason remembered reading about the man in the newspapers of the time. Reading about him and coming to hate him. Until the hate was too much to bear and he forgot him.

"You said all the evidence proved my mother guilty," Jason said harshly.

"I did. Again and again," Morgan said.

"You called her a cold-blooded murderer. You said she deserved death."

"I did."

"Then what do you want of me now?" Jason asked.

The man didn't speak.

"What?" Jason asked again, and there was fierce anger and bitterness in his voice.

The man had lowered his head, and now he slowly raised it and looked at Jason, his face tight with anguish.

"Do you believe in God?" he asked.

"God?"

"Do you?" Morgan said.

"No. Why should I?"

"Why should you?" the man said sadly.

40

Jason's voice rose when he spoke again. "Give me a good reason. One. Even one."

Morgan shook his head. "I can't. You'll have to find it yourself."

"Sure. In this beautiful and just world," Jason said bitterly. "I'll find it. Do you really believe that?"

He turned away, and there was a hint of tears in the gray eyes.

"Jason."

And then he heard the man say in a whisper, "I do believe. And I believe that I will burn in hell. Unless. . . ."

The voice faded out.

"Unless what?" Jason asked harshly.

"Unless you help me prove that I was wrong."

"Wrong?"

"That your mother was not guilty," Morgan said.

"What?"

"Yes. Before they kill her."

Jason stared at the man.

"We have only a few days left to do that," Morgan continued.

"Not guilty?" Jason whispered.

"Yes."

Jason came close to the man. "What kind of a horrible joke are you pulling on me?" he suddenly shouted.

His voice was like a fist.

The man flinched backward and raised his frail hand to his face fearfully.

"Haven't I been tortured enough?" Jason shouted.

"Please. Please listen to me," Morgan said.

"No. I've had enough. Enough." And Jason turned abruptly to walk out of the room and into the cooling, healing night.

"You talk of hell. Of burning there. That's where you belong," he said bitterly.

His hand was on the doorknob.

But then he heard the desperate, pleading voice. "You have a chance to save your mother. To save her."

41

Jason slowly turned back to the man.

"Don't walk out on it. Don't. It will be on your conscience for the rest of your life. Don't do it, son," Morgan begged.

Jason stood still, his hands trembling.

"Listen, Jason. Please. When the sentence of death was passed on me, I started to think of Marian Feldon. Of her sentence of death."

The man shuddered in pain and paused.

"Don't go, Jason. Please." He closed his eyes and leaned back against the chair. And with the blue anguished eyes closed, the face looked like that of a cadaver.

Then the eyes slowly opened again.

The thin lips started with a whisper, and then the voice grew stronger.

"I began to think of her. And to see her in my mind. I began to sit in the cell with Marian Feldon. Day after day. Hour after hour. I remembered again and again her shouting that I was framing her. Everybody was framing her. Everybody."

He paused again.

Jason waited.

"I began to take another look at the evidence I had collected. To look at it from the other side of the telescope. From her side. It made me ask new questions. Questions nobody had asked before."

There were now gleaming drops of perspiration on the pale forehead.

"And the more I probed, the more I saw that there were people. Powerful, ruthless people who didn't want the truth to get out."

"Why?" Jason whispered.

He now stood over the man, his face white and taut.

"Because one of them murdered Arthur Madison. And the other ordered the killing. Your mother came into the room that night, and Madison was already dead. As she always claimed."

"She was found with the gun in her hand," Jason said.

"The killer's gun. She had picked it up. It was all a frame," Morgan said.

He paused and looked up at Jason. "You're starting to believe me."

"Yes," Jason said.

"Madison was a heavy gambler. A secret one. Nobody knew that. He welshed on his debts. He was killed."

Morgan reached for the glass of water and then raised it to his lips and sipped slowly, thirstily. His hand shook.

Jason saw how weak and spent the man was.

But Morgan went on, as if by naked will alone.

"I fell for the frame. Why? Because deep inside me I wanted to. I know that now."

"Wanted to?"

The man nodded. "Yes."

"Why? What did my mother ever do to you?"

"Nothing, Jason. Nothing."

He was silent for a moment, and then he spoke again.

"I hated all women at that time. My wife had a lover. My respectable wife. Your respectable mother had a lover. I hated her. Maybe I was striking out at my wife through your mother. Do you understand that?"

Jason didn't answer.

"Hatred blinds you. I blinded myself and fell for the frame. And then helped it along."

He paused and looked up at Jason.

"Do you think God will ever forgive me for that? Will your mother? Will you?" There were tears in the man's eyes.

Jason was still silent.

"Will you, Jason?"

Jason wanted to reach out and touch the man, but he stood there, not moving, his shadow dark on the floor.

Morgan turned away and stared hopelessly out the window and into the night.

"You'll never forgive me," he said in a hoarse whisper. "Nor will Marian Feldon. No matter what I do."

He sighed, then slowly, painfully, turned back to Jason.

"I have all the new evidence in a file. But before I could

43

do anything with it, I collapsed. I was flown up here to try and save my life. It's no use, I'm going to die. But your mother must not. Do you hear me, Jason? She must not die.''

He coughed and leaned forward.

''You're the only one I can trust to do it. The only one.''

''To do what?'' Jason asked.

''To get the file and bring it here.''

''Where is it?''

''Locked away in a small safe. In my house. Will you do it?''

''You say it will help save my mother?''

The man slowly nodded. ''Yes. I'm sure of it.''

''I'll go,'' Jason said.

Morgan's lips quivered, and Jason thought he was about to cry.

''Fly down tomorrow,'' he murmured. ''Every day counts.''

Then he turned and pointed to a bureau in the corner of the room.

''The top drawer.''

Jason looked at him and then went over to the bureau and opened the drawer.

''An envelope,'' Morgan directed.

Jason found the envelope and brought it over to Morgan.

''My house keys. The safe combination. My address.''

Jason took the envelope from him and put it away in the inside pocket of his jacket.

''Good.''

Morgan leaned back in his chair and closed his eyes and rested, and then he spoke again.

''It's off-season now. You'll be able to get a plane.''

''I'll get one,'' Jason said.

Morgan smiled, a wan smile, yet it made his face look young for an instant.

''The second drawer,'' he said.

Jason went over and opened the drawer.

''Under the blue shirt. Another envelope.''

Jason found the envelope and brought it over to Morgan.

"There's eleven hundred dollars in it. Check it."

Jason looked in the envelope and counted the money.

"Eleven hundred," he said.

"Take it and use it when you have to."

Jason put the envelope in his pocket.

"Do you drive?" Morgan asked.

"Yes," he said.

"I knew you did. Just checking it out."

The man smiled again. "I know more about you then you know about yourself. Don't fly into Fort Myers. There's a chance they'll be watching the airport. Take a plane to Lauderdale. There'll be a man named John Eagan waiting for you."

"John Eagan?"

"Tall. About six foot two. Gray hair. A tiny scar on his left cheek. He used to work for me."

"I'll try to get the morning plane out," Jason said.

"Eastern. If you don't get it, call me here and tell me the plane you're taking."

"Okay."

"Eagan will have a car ready for you to drive across to the Gulf side. He'll know you. But he doesn't know anything else."

Morgan looked long and silently at Jason, and then he leaned back and sighed low.

"It's just you and I, Jason. Your mother lives or dies with us."

Jason didn't speak.

Then he heard Morgan again.

"Help me to my bed. I'm very tired."

Jason went over and then helped the man walk slowly across the room to his bed.

"Thanks, Jason," Morgan whispered. "Turn out the light."

The darkness of the night now came into the room.

But in its corner a night-light glowed.

The man lay in the bed, silent and alone.

Finally, he spoke.

"Watch yourself. This is a deadly game you're in."

"I know," Jason said.

"You don't. They're killers. They know what I've been doing. They know their lives are now on the line. They know, Jason."

Jason was silent.

"Trust nobody. Tell nobody. You're the one they'll least suspect. That's why I'm sending you and not John Eagan. You understand that?"

"Yes."

"Promise you won't tell anybody."

"I won't."

"Promise."

"I promise," Jason said.

"On your mother's life."

Jason looked through the darkness to the stern face with the tight, bloodless lips.

"On my mother's life," Jason said.

"I believe you now."

The eyes of the man gleamed.

"Get the file and bring it back here. I have to sign the documents. And then you'll take them to Todman."

"Walter Todman?"

"Yes. He'll get your mother a stay of execution. I'm sure that he will."

"And after that?" Jason asked.

"Her freedom."

"You're sure of that, too?"

"Yes, Jason. It was my testimony that sent her to a death cell. Now my testimony and proof of new evidence will take her out of it."

"I'll get the file," Jason said.

"Good."

Morgan closed his eyes. Again his face looked like that of a cadaver.

And then Jason heard his voice whispering through the stillness.

"Jason."

"Yes?"

"Do you think God will forgive me?"

Jason didn't answer.

"When Marian Feldon and you forgive me . . . then he will," Morgan said.

"She'll forgive you," Jason said.

The eyes were still closed.

The thin lips shut.

"And I will, too," Jason said.

But he didn't know if the man heard him.

Jason quietly left the room.

Chapter

14

He bought the tickets for the morning's flight at the airline terminal on Forty-second Street, and then he went down into the subway and took the train to Brooklyn Heights. Carla was waiting for him at their favorite spot on the Esplanade.

They began walking in the darkness, looking out at the distant wavering lights of Manhattan and down at the boats in the river.

He watched a black tugboat guide a freighter away from its slip and out into the mainstream of the river.

"You're not talking much tonight," Carla said.

He shrugged, and then began walking again.

"Something on my mind," he said.

She looked up at him and said quietly, "There's always something on your mind, Jason."

"Is there?"

"Yes."

"It's my temperament," he said. "I'm a quiet guy."

"You are."

"I guess I'm not much good company."

"Now or always?"

"Always."

She shook her head. "I wouldn't say that."

"But you'd like it if I spoke more."

"No. I take life as it comes, Jason. You come along this way, so I take you this way."

"And you're happy with it."

"I'm happy," Carla said.

He smiled and put his arm around her.

"That's better," she said.

"Okay."

He kissed her gently on her fragrant hair. She pressed his hand, and they walked on, close to each other.

"Carla," he said.

"Yes?"

He hesitated and then spoke. "I have to go away early in the morning. I hope to be back very late at night. Or maybe the next day."

"And?"

"I'm telling Lydia that I'm going to be with you."

"With me?"

"Yes."

She stopped walking, drew away, and looked up at him.

"What do you mean?" she asked.

"Just trust me."

"I don't get it."

"I'm telling her that we're going up to your uncle's cabin in Ellenville. We've done that before," Jason said.

"But we've told her before."

"I know."

"I still don't get it, Jason."

"You'll be doing me a great favor," he said.

"You'll have to tell me why."

He looked away from her direct gaze.

"I can't."

"Why can't you, Jason?"

"Carla, will you just—?"

"If you're involving me, I'd like to know why," she cut in.

49

"Lydia, don't crowd me," he said bitterly.

"I'm not Lydia."

He sighed.

"You're not. Okay, so you won't do it," he said.

"I didn't say that."

"But . . ."

She came close to him again. "Jason."

"Yes?"

She put her hand gently on his, and the touch was cold to him. "Listen to me."

"Go on."

When she spoke again, her voice was low and tentative. "I don't know why, but somehow you're starting to scare me."

"What do you mean?"

"It's a weird feeling that's just come over me."

"Carla."

And he saw an intense and searching look in her eyes. "I mean it, Jason. Scared. And I don't scare easily."

"Carla, stop this."

She shook her head. "No. It came over me when you called me Lydia."

He didn't speak.

She spoke, and her voice was low and trembling.

"You can say it's a slip. A Freudian slip. But it's something even deeper than that, Jason. I feel that something is wrong with you. Very wrong."

"Nothing."

"I can feel it. Deep inside of me," she said.

"Nothing's wrong, I said."

She shook her head fiercely. "No. I've been wanting to get this out of me for a long time."

He looked coldly at her. "Leave it alone, Carla."

"No. It's been with me too long. Almost as long as I've known you."

"Carla," he said, and his voice was loud and harsh.

But she went on. "Lately I feel . . . I don't know how to describe it. . . ."

Her words trailed away into the night silence. "I don't, Jason."

She looked at him helplessly and then went over to a bench and slowly sat down on it.

The light of the street lamp was full upon her, making her look small and vulnerable.

She stared into the night, her face pale, her lips quivering.

And he saw how much she cared for him.

His heart went out to her.

He wanted to go over and take her into his arms and comfort her.

But he stood there, not moving.

Then he heard her speak again.

"Jason, sometimes you get a look in your eyes, a deep and lost look, and I feel that you're mourning, in your heart you're mourning for somebody."

He stared silently at her.

"Like somebody close to you is dying."

"Dying?" he whispered.

"Yes, Jason. Yes."

He turned abruptly away from her.

"Leave it alone, Carla. Just leave it alone."

"You won't tell me?" she asked.

"There's nothing to tell."

She had risen, and now they stood facing each other.

Out on the river a boat whistle sounded, and then all was quiet again.

"Okay," she said. "There's nothing."

"Let's call it a night," he said.

They walked back without saying another word.

Chapter

15

On the subway train back to Manhattan, at the Fourteenth Street station, a man came into the nearly empty car and sat down next to Jason. He was elderly, well-dressed, and he had a trim white mustache.

"You look sad, young fellow."

Jason didn't say anything.

"That's all right. I'm sad, too. But it's all inside. Learned to keep it hidden inside. You get on better with people that way," the man said.

He smiled. He had blue eyes, blue young eyes, and Jason thought instantly of Morgan. Morgan, who lay dying in a strange hospital bed. More than a thousand miles from home.

"You have to get on with people," the man continued, "or you'll never be successful. I'm retired now. And I've been successful. Get on with people. That's the slogan. Talk to people and get on with them. You have a father?"

"No," Jason said.

"Dead?"

"He's dead."

"A long time?"

"Yes," Jason said.

The man suddenly became silent and didn't speak again until the next station came up.

And what he said startled Jason.

"I gave you a bad world, didn't I?"

"What?"

"My generation. We gave you nothing but trouble and heartache. No future. Isn't that so?"

"I don't know."

"But you do know. That's why you're so sad."

Jason shrugged silently.

"All of you are sad," the man said. "Just listen to the songs you sing. Sad, sad, sad. Isn't that so?"

"Maybe."

The man had a low resonant voice. "And my generation is a bunch of blowhards. That's what they are. We give you a lot of happy talk. And we wave flags. We don't want to face up to the horrors and devastation we handed down to you. There's no hope for you anywhere, is there?"

He turned to get closer to Jason, and as he did, Jason saw that a good part of the man's right arm was missing. The lower end of the tailored sleeve was empty.

The man saw Jason looking at the empty sleeve, and he smiled.

"Lost it in the war. The big one. But there's another one coming, isn't there? The biggest bang of them all."

The smile was gone from the delicate lips.

"An absurd world. Just absurd. It's becoming a tale told by an idiot and listened to by idiots. Am I right?"

Jason didn't answer.

"Well, am I?" The man's eyes were now cold, like little points of blue steel.

"Yes," Jason murmured.

The train was coming into the Thirty-fourth Street station, and the man got up and started for the doors.

Then he turned and looked back to Jason.

"Don't listen to us blowhards. Don't. Go on and make

your own world. It couldn't be worse than the one we made. Could it?''

Then he suddenly said, his face pale and tight, "But it's no matter. You're going to die young. I can see it on you. You're marked for death.''

The doors closed, and he vanished.

But Jason still heard the voice.

"You're marked for death.''

Chapter

16

Lydia was asleep when he got back to the apartment, so he wrote a note and left it on the kitchen table, where she was sure to find it. Then he went into his room, closed the door, and undressed.

He lay on the white bed, his eyes wide open. The moonlight coming through the window silvered one of the walls of the room, giving it a ghostly pallor.

He lay there for hours, thinking, ever thinking.

Toward morning, he dozed.

The alarm woke him, and he sat up in bed, shivering. Yet the room was warm.

"Carla," he whispered, and he didn't know why he did that.

But deep, deep within him he ached to hold her in his arms again and never to wake.

Soon he got up and dressed.

Then he went to Lydia's door and opened it and looked in.

She was still asleep.

He went over to the bed and looked down at her face.

It was peaceful and serene.

At that instant, she looked so very much like his mother, except for the bleak sadness that was ever with Marian Feldon.

Jason picked up the small bottle of pills that stood on Lydia's night table. Lately, she had started to use pills to help her sleep.

He wondered if she had increased the dosage.

The days were passing too fast.

Much, much too fast.

Or are they too slow for you, Lydia?

Each minute that you think of your condemned sister becomes an hour of brutal torture to you.

Each minute brings you closer to her execution.

To my mother's death.

Time, Lydia, time has us both by the throat.

Jason looked again at the sleeping face, and then he reached down and gently, tenderly, stroked Lydia's hair.

You've been good to me, he thought.

So very good.

I never would have made it up to now without you.

Chances are I would've killed myself.

Yes.

He stopped stroking her hair, and her eyes opened.

She looked at him, but there was no recognition.

An expression of terror was deep within her eyes.

Naked terror.

Her lips opened, and she whispered something he could not make out.

It had a desperate pleading tone to it.

The trembling lips whispered jumbled words again.

And then the eyes and lips closed, and she slept.

Jason turned and went silently out of the room and then out of the apartment.

He was alone in the elevator.

He was alone in the lobby.

When he got out of the building and onto the sidewalk, the morning was bright and crisp. He stood on the pavement and stared about him. It was very early, and the city was just starting to come awake.

Then, he didn't know why, something told him to look up.

He did and was startled to see the dark form of Lydia standing at the terrace railing.

Her face small and white.

Her eyes looking directly down at him.

"Lydia," he murmured.

He waved to her.

He was positive that she saw him, but she just stood there, motionless.

Looking down at him.

He slowly turned and started to walk away from her, and it was then that he heard her cry.

"Jason!"

It cut through the air to him.

Agonized and piercing.

"Jason!"

He did not turn.

He just kept walking on, wondering if he would ever see her again.

Chapter

17

The cabdriver was silent all the way to the airport. Just as Jason leaned over to pay him, he started to speak.

"My wife said to me this morning, 'You're going to have a bad day. You'll be robbed. And maybe killed.' And she never says such things to me. She had a bad dream. She didn't want me to go out this morning. To stay home. It's on my mind now. What do you think? Should I knock it off and go home?"

Jason gave him the money, and he gave Jason the change. Jason gave him a tip.

"Thanks. What do you think? You're my first fare."

"I don't know," Jason said.

"I don't know, either. That's why I'm asking you."

"Go home," Jason said.

"You think so?"

"Yes."

The cabdriver sat there. He had an old and worn face. "I sound stupid to you?" he asked.

"No. You don't."

"You look young and bright. And sad. There's a sad look

on your face, and it's so early in the morning. Why are you sad? I'm old and tired and scared. I've been driving too long. The wife wants me to give it all up. Should I?''

"Maybe you should," Jason said.

"Maybe I should." He nodded thoughtfully. "It's not what it used to be. People are killing people in this city. For a nickel. It's not what it used to be. Maybe I should listen to you and go home and stay in the house."

People are killing people, Jason thought.

"Maybe I'll listen to you," the cabdriver said.

And then he waved at Jason and drove off.

Jason walked slowly into the airport building.

People are killing people.

Chapter
18

Just before boarding the plane, he stopped, got out of the line, and then hurried over to a phone booth and called Carla.

He wanted desperately to hear her voice.

Just that.

Just that and he would hang up.

Just to hear her say, "Hello?" and nothing more.

That's all he wanted.

It was so little to want.

Her father answered.

He heard her father's voice.

"She's not home, Jason."

"Oh."

"She might be back in a half hour."

"A half hour?"

"Yes. Better call then."

"I won't be able to," Jason said.

"Tied up?"

"Yes, Mr. Swenson."

"That's too bad."

"It is."

"I'm sure she'd like to speak to you."

He didn't speak.

"Anywhere she can reach you?"

"No, Mr. Swenson."

And he stood there watching the moving line, holding the phone with a tight grip.

"Do you want to leave a message?"

"I guess not, Mr. Swenson."

"Should I tell her you called?"

"Yes."

"Just that?"

"Uh-huh."

There was a pause, and then he heard the man speak again. This time in a very gentle, almost tentative voice.

"Jason?"

"Yes?"

"Carla was crying when she came home last night."

"Crying?"

"She never cries."

"I know," Jason said.

"Anything wrong with the two of you?" Mr. Swenson asked.

"No."

"Are you sure?"

Jason didn't answer.

"Want to talk to me, Jason? I'm sure I'll understand."

"There's nothing wrong, Mr. Swenson."

There was a slight pause, and Jason thought he could hear the man sigh.

"Okay, then. I'll tell her you called."

"Thanks. Good-bye, Mr. Swenson."

"Good-bye, Jason."

He slowly put the receiver back onto its hook.

Then he turned and ran for the plane.

All the time seeing the tears in Carla's eyes.

And feeling his heart heavy within him.

Chapter

19

Most of the time he sat looking out the window at the sun-filled sky, all the way to Fort Lauderdale.

And memories came flooding back to him.

One persisted.

He was sitting in his sociology class, and the discussion topic of the day was capital punishment.

When the instructor, Mr. Cahn, announced the subject, Jason wanted to get up and walk out of the classroom. But he had held himself in with a tight rein and sat there and listened.

Everybody had a chance to express a point of view.

Finally, Mr. Cahn called on him.

"I have no opinion," he said.

"But you must, Jason."

The two liked and admired each other.

Jason shook his head silently.

"But this is a subject that the whole country is interested in. It's reported in the newspapers and on television. It's a very important issue."

"I'm sure it is."

"Everybody has an opinion on capital punishment."

"I don't."

"Jason."

"I've nothing to say on it."

The instructor came closer to him and spoke gently and persuasively.

"You've heard the pros and cons. I think we've had a fine and stimulating discussion. Don't you want to add to it?"

"I'd rather not," Jason said.

"Any particular reasons?"

"None."

"I can't understand why you're so stubborn on the matter." He put his hand gently on Jason's shoulder. "Jason, you have an excellent mind, and you do have opinions."

The rest of the class watched silently.

"I said I have none."

"I won't accept that."

"I'm afraid you'll have to, Mr. Cahn."

"You're questioning my authority before the entire class."

"I guess I am," Jason said.

The instructor's face paled, and then his voice became cold and commanding.

"I want you to speak up. Even if it's only for a few words. I insist on that, Jason."

"A few words," Jason said quietly.

Mr. Cahn nodded grimly.

Jason looked at all of them.

And suddenly it came out with a rush from within him, all of his bitterness and his agony, his mother's bleak eyes ever before him.

"All right," he said. "I'll tell you what I think about it. Capital punishment is savage and cruel and inhuman. You torture a person like you do a caught fly. You tear off the wings one by one, and then you spout great and civilized reasons for doing so. You even have the gall to take the name of God and say that he approves of what you do. God gives and takes lives. Not you, you monsters. Not you, you hypocrites. Not you, you liars. Did it ever come into your uncivilized minds that you are inflicting horrible pain and severe punishment on the innocent family and their loved ones? Did it ever come into your closed minds that you might be murdering an innocent person? And what do you do when you find out the truth too late? You murderers, do you bring her back to life? Can you?''

He paused, and everybody in the classroom was looking at him with white faces.

''In a word, I think capital punishment stinks.''

Jason turned and walked out of the room.

Mr. Cahn's head was bowed.

Then he said in a low and almost inaudible voice, ''Class is dismissed.''

Chapter

20

What do you do when you murder an innocent woman?

Can you bring her back to life?

Can you?

Jason's hands clenched and unclenched.

"Coffee?"

He turned and looked up into the stewardess's smiling face.

"Why are you smiling?" Jason asked.

"Because I'm paid to." She poured him a cup of coffee. "And also because it's a beautiful day."

"I guess it is," he said.

"You're handsome," she said. "Come around when you're a bit older."

"Okay, I will."

They both laughed.

And then he looked out the window again.

Chapter

21

He had taken no luggage, so when the plane landed, he walked directly to the lobby of the airport. No one was there to greet him.

No one.

He found an empty chair and sat down and waited.

He studied every person passing through the lobby, the tension within him steadily growing.

And the fears.

What if the man never shows up? he said to himself.

What then?

What do I do?

The doubts crowded in on him, giving him no rest.

This is all madness, he said to himself.

Sheer madness.

There are no documents.

Face the harsh truth.

Face it.

Your mother is guilty, and she's going to die.

Marian Feldon is guilty.

Even her own lawyer says so.

All the rest is nothing but sick illusion.

Sick.

Morgan is sick and dying, and he doesn't know what he's saying.

He's fooling himself, and he's fooling you.

Jason, it's nothing but illusion.

He felt it impossible to sit any longer. He was about to get up and walk restlessly around the bleak lobby.

Outside it had begun to rain, a heavy, dreary rain.

They'll take my mother out to die on a day like this, he thought bitterly.

"Sing me a death song, Jason."

A death song.

Suddenly a tall man with gray hair and a tiny scar on his cheek sat down on the chair next to him.

Jason trembled and held his breath.

The man had a newspaper in his large hand. He slowly, precisely, opened it and began reading.

Jason waited tensely.

The minutes went by slowly, ever so slowly.

Jason stared out the heavy, plate-glass window at the dreary sky.

And suddenly he heard the man speak, in a low but clear voice.

"You're Jason Ross."

"Yes."

"I'm John Eagan."

Jason was about to turn to him when Eagan said quietly, "Don't. Just keep looking about you. But not at me."

He stopped speaking and concentrated again on the newspaper.

The large hand slowly turned the pages.

Then the man spoke again:

"Listen closely. When I'm finished talking, you go out to the parking lot. Section A2. There's a black Honda Accord with a small dent on the right front fender. It's near the head of the left lane. Two cars away."

He paused.

A woman came over and sat next to him.

He read his newspaper.

Finally, the woman got up and went over to the other end of the lobby, his sharp eyes following her.

Jason heard the voice again. "The keys and registration papers are in the glove compartment. Look at your watch if you read me so far."

Jason glanced at his watch.

"Good. Now remember this. Take care when you get over to the other side. Frank Morgan has made some bad enemies there. He sent you to do something for him. Do it and get out as fast and as quietly as you can. I'll be sitting here tomorrow morning. Waiting for you. Now don't get up yet. Wait. And then go for the car. Slowly. Leisurely."

He paused. "Don't look back."

Jason sat there, waiting tensely, and then finally he rose.

He heard the man's voice again. "Be careful."

Jason walked slowly out of the airport lobby and into the rain.

He stood looking about him until he saw the parking lot.

"A2," he murmured.

He found the section, and then he ran through the lines of wet, glistening cars until he came to the black Honda with the dent on the front fender.

He sighed.

Then he got into the car, opened the glove compartment, and took out the keys.

Jason turned on the motor and sat there getting his breath back.

There is a John Eagan, he said to himself.

There is.

He drove off through the rain and onto the highway.

Chapter

22

He remembered the words of a Langston Hughes poem.

Bear in mind
That Death is a drum.
A drum.
A drum.

And in his fevered mind he changed the words to:

Death beats a drum.
A drum.
A drum.
Death beats a drum.
A drum.
A drum.

The sound of the windshield wipers repeated the words in a cold and insistent rhythm.

Death beats a drum.
A drum.
A drum.

He stopped the wipers.

And yet he still heard the words in the same obsessive rhythm.

The windows streamed with the rain until it was hard to see.

He put on the wipers again.

Death beats a drum.
A drum.
A drum.

Jason pulled over to the shoulder of the highway and turned off the motor.

He sat there a long while, his eyes closed.

Finally, he opened his eyes and started the car again and drove onto the highway.

He put on the windshield wipers again.

The death rhythm was gone.

The sound was now a soothing one.

He sighed in peace.

Chapter

23

When he came to Orlando, it was still raining heavily. He drove through to the other side of the city, and he realized, as he stopped for a red light, that he was very hungry and tired. He rode along until he saw a McDonald's, and then he parked the car in the empty, rain-swept lot and went inside and ordered a hamburger and coffee.

The place was deserted and quiet.

"And some french fries."

"French fries," the girl behind the counter said in a light and cheery voice. "We make the best fries in all Florida."

Her eyes were smiling at him.

"Do you?"

She was about his age, blond and attractive.

"That's right. We Disnefy them," she said.

"Disnefy?" And he laughed.

"It's a magic method. McDonald's stole it from Disneyland."

He listened to her, and it put a warm feeling in him. She reminded him of Carla when she laughed.

It would have been good to have Carla with me now, he

thought. It would have made things easier. I wouldn't feel so alone. So fearful and alone.

"You live around here?" the girl asked.

"No, I don't."

He liked her, and he felt that she liked him.

"Visiting Disneyland?" she asked.

"No."

"Epcot? That more your style?"

He shook his head and smiled at the girl. "Just driving through."

"Oh." She was putting his order together. "Going far?"

"Pretty far."

"Coming back this way?"

"I hope to," he said.

"Well, then drop in. I'm always here at this time."

"Sure thing," he said.

She handed him his tray, and their hands touched.

"Have a good day," she said.

"I'm trying to."

"The rain's not helping any, is it?"

"It sure isn't."

They both laughed, and then he took the tray, went over to a table, and sat down.

The table was by a window that overlooked the parking lot. His car stood alone in the rain. Black and silent.

He ate slowly and thoughtfully.

In his mind he went over the route he was taking. Once he got over to the Gulf side, he would go down the coast through Sarasota and then on and through Fort Myers and from there turn in and make his way to Thornton.

The city of Thornton.

His eyes grew dark and bitter.

He remembered the huge billboards that stood flanking the highway on the outskirts of the city.

The big printed letters and the garish sunshine colors.

Welcome to the Golden City of Thornton.

Nestling on the waters of the sparkling Gulf.

Our climate is the best.

72

Our golf courses prime.

Our schools rank highest in the state.

Marian Feldon, our superintendent, is a noted and respected educator.

Her standards are the highest.

None higher and better in the whole state.

Come on down with your children and settle here.

They'll get a better education here than anywhere else.

They will.

We guarantee that.

Marian Feldon, winner of many honors and awards, will see to that.

She sure will!

So come on down!

There was no intersection on the highway at that point, but there was a red light that stopped traffic every four minutes so that people in the cars would have enough time to sit and read the billboards.

Oh, how proud Thornton was of Marian Feldon.

Jason smiled grimly.

He wondered what the billboards would be saying now, whether they were still there.

And then he thought of the man who had the boards put up.

Arthur Madison.

Prominent and influential lawyer.

A bachelor who always lived a model and socially committed life.

A man of good deeds, all of his years.

His shortened years.

Jason put down his coffee cup and stared somberly at it.

For he was listening again to the prosecutor's voice ringing through the crowded and silent courtroom.

Marian Feldon and Arthur Madison, he shouted.

Two names.

Two names eternally linked together.

Ill-fated people.

One destined to be innocently murdered in cold blood and the other to be justly executed.

I repeat, executed.

Executed.

The prosecutor paused and then looked sternly at the white faces of the jury.

He raised his hand high and shouted again.

Executed justly, I say.

I say it again and again.

Justly.

Justly.

Justly.

He turned and walked slowly over to his chair and sat down.

Then he spoke again in a harsh and level voice.

For we are in a court of justice, are we not?

"A court of justice," Jason whispered bitterly.

He looked through the window at the blurring rain and then saw something that turned him cold and taut.

A dark figure was standing by the Honda.

Jason watched intently.

The man bent over the front door and began working on the lock with a small tool that gleamed in the rain.

Jason rose and hurried out of the restaurant.

"Hey!" he shouted.

He ran to the car.

The man straightened up and faced Jason. "What's wrong?"

"That's my car," Jason said fiercely.

"Is it?"

He was stocky and had a tight face and hard black eyes. The rain dripped down over his lean cheeks.

"You're trying to get into my car," Jason said.

The man looked quietly and calmly at Jason.

"It's yours?"

"Yes."

"You sure about it?"

"Of course I am. Just drove it from Lauderdale."

"Lauderdale?"

The man's eyes glistened.

"Yes. What are you trying to pull on me?"

"Nothing, kid. Nothing. I guess I made a mistake." He grinned and then abruptly turned and walked away into the rain.

Jason stood watching him disappear, and then he turned back to the car and examined the door.

The lock had been opened.

Jason stood there, the rain sweeping down upon him.

Then he slowly got into the car and drove off leaving behind him the unfinished meal.

Chapter

24

He drove along, his clothes wet and cold.

The chill went deep inside him.

The chill of fear.

What did the man really want?

Who was he?

A car thief?

Just figured he'd take off with the Honda and get rid of it?

Sell it?

Have it chopped up and sell the parts?

Was that it?

Or is he somebody else?

With another reason?

A deadly one.

Watch yourself, Morgan had said.

These people know their lives are on the line.

They know it, Jason.

Be careful, John Eagan had said.

Those were his last words.

Be careful.

Chapter

25

It was late afternoon when he came to Fort Myers. He drove through the town and then turned down the beach highway. The rain had stopped, and the sun, the south Florida sun that he had once loved so much, came out and flooded the sky with a gentle warmth and glow.

His eyes scanned the beaches and the white sand as he drove along, and then the memory came back to him, clear and strong.

He was sitting on the beach between his mother and Lydia.

He was very young.

And yet he remembered them talking to each other.

Lydia had come down from New York to stay a week with them.

"You shouldn't see him anymore, Marian."

"Why not?" his mother asked.

"Because he's not good for you."

"I'll be the judge of that, Lydia."

Lydia turned to help Jason fill his pail with sand, and then she said in a low voice, "I just don't trust him, that's all."

"You're wrong, Lydia."

"I think he's all facade. Underneath he's nothing but a—"

And Marian cut in furiously. "Phony?" she said.

"You said it," Lydia answered.

"And you were about to say it."

"Then I'll say it. He's a self-centered fraud. Out for himself and only himself. And you'll end up with a lot of grief."

"I wish you wouldn't lecture me, Lydia."

"I'm not lecturing you. Just trying to help you."

"I wish you wouldn't try to help me, Lydia."

"Then I won't."

Lydia turned to Jason and tenderly brushed his hair back with her hand, and then she reached over and kissed him.

Jason remembered the warmth and love in the kiss.

An almost desperate, hungry love.

Lydia had never married.

"People are talking about the two of you, Marian," she said.

"Let them talk. He's a bachelor, and I'm a widow. What's so very wrong in our relationship?" his mother asked.

"You're a school superintendent. A role model. Superintendents marry. They do not have open affairs."

"Open?"

"Everybody can see it," Lydia said.

"Let them."

"Marian, this is not New York where you can do as you please. It's Thornton. Where everybody watches what everybody does."

"Let them watch."

Lydia turned and dumped Jason's pail over with a gay cry and then laughed with him.

"Oh, what did I do? Now we'll have to fill another one," she said.

She hugged him close.

"I don't like where this is going, Marian. It's worrying me."

"Where is it going?"

"To a bad end. He can't be trusted. He'll break your heart."

"I can take care of myself."

"You can't. You're too impulsive. You'll do something that will . . ." She didn't finish.

"Let's leave this alone," Marian said. "I've had enough."

"All right. If that's what you want."

"That's exactly what I want, Lydia."

Then Jason remembered that the two sisters were grimly silent, and he played quietly and looked out at the sea.

The sun glowed on the broad reach of blue water.

Just as it was doing now.

Jason started to shovel more sand into the pail when he heard his mother suddenly speak in a low and harsh voice.

"How is it you know so much about Arthur Madison?" she asked.

"How?"

"Yes, Lydia." His mother's face was white and taut.

"Just what are you implying, Marian?"

"I'm asking you a direct question, and you're not answering me."

"Are you saying that I've been seeing Arthur?" Lydia asked.

"You're still not answering me," his mother said.

"Or that I used to go with him in the past?"

"Lydia."

"Let's say my knowledge of his character comes from womanly intuition," Lydia said.

"Intuition, no less."

"Yes, Marian."

The two looked at each other silently.

Like two bitter enemies, Jason thought.

And there was fear in his heart.

For he loved the two of them.

Marian stood up.

"I think we'd better get back to the house. It's too chilly here," she said.

"It is."

Lydia helped Jason get his playthings together.

"Are you angry, Lydia?" he asked.

"No, Jason."

And then Jason remembered her saying in a low voice, almost to herself, "Just scared."

All the way back to the house the two sisters didn't speak to each other.

Chapter
26

He stopped to get gas, and as he stood by his car, waiting for the tank to be filled, he heard a voice close to him.

"How's it going, kid?"

Jason turned and looked into the lean face of the man who had tried to steal his car.

"You got down here all right, didn't you?" The man smiled.

Jason didn't answer.

"I know you're angry at me, kid. And you have every right to be. But I was stuck on the road with no car, and I thought I'd borrow yours."

"Borrow?"

"Sure. And then get it back to you." The man grinned at him.

"I'm sure you would have," Jason said.

"I'd find you. I'm good at finding people," the man said.

"Yes, I guess you are."

"I found you here, didn't I?"

"You did."

"No hard feelings?"

Jason looked quietly at him and said nothing.

The man put his hand out. "I'm Ed Carter. You going in to Thornton? I could use a lift."

"No," Jason said, not taking his hand. "I'm going down to Naples."

"Well, that's on the way. How about it?"

Jason shook his head grimly.

"Find somebody else," he said.

"Won't take me?"

"No."

"C'mon, have a heart. I've just come out of Colby Prison," the man said.

"Colby?" Jason paled.

"I've done my time. Paid my debt. Have a heart."

Colby was where Marian Feldon was to be executed.

"So you're turning me down. Okay," the man said. He grinned at Jason, and there was a sardonic, mocking look in his hard black eyes.

He turned and walked away onto the shoulder of the highway. Jason watched him until he disappeared in the haze.

And all the time he felt a cold terror within him.

As if he had picked up a snake in his hand.

Chapter

27

He decided that he wouldn't go into Thornton until it was quite dark. So he parked the black Honda on a deserted beach and then walked over to a rocky ledge and sat down and gazed out at the sea.

Slowly and softly, the horizon began to redden.

The sun began to sink into the water, slowly, inevitably.

Jason's eyes saddened.

The bright, bright sun is beginning to die, he said to himself.

Its blood is streaming over the sea.

Every day it dies.

And the world dies with it.

Leaving nothing behind but death, death, and again death.

Nothing but that.

He put his fist to his mouth to keep from crying out.

He sat there a long while on the ledge, not moving.

At last, an evening breeze came up and rippled the smooth and level water, and then he watched a spray of glimmering white foam float lazily in to the shore.

All became vastly still.

Except for the gentle murmur of the tiny waves.

Jason breathed out, and a strange inner peace began to spread within him. Strange and soothing.

And now he saw with clear, unclouded eyes the great beauty of the fading sunset.

Saw only that.

He sat back and let the soft wind play with his hair and cool his warm forehead.

The thought of the Esplanade and of Carla floated gently in to him.

"Carla," he whispered.

And he imagined himself sitting quietly and contentedly with Carla at his side, his arm about her shoulder, her warm cheek close to his.

Carla.

The sky slowly began to darken.

The wind grew a bit stronger.

A page of a newspaper blew across the sand, rocked crazily up and then down, and landed at his feet.

It lay there.

Flat and silent.

Waiting for the next thrust of wind to pick it up and take it away from Jason.

He looked down and glanced at it.

The *Thornton Daily News*.

Jason bent over and picked up the paper.

He brushed away the sand, and then he saw the column headed by the words "Marian Feldon to Die Friday."

Her picture.

He looked into her dark and bleak eyes, and they seemed to speak to him.

Jason.

Jason, my only son.

Save me.

Jason.

Friday is so close.

So frighteningly close.

Time is going too fast, he said to himself desperately.

Every minute is starting to count.

Every single second.

He closed his eyes to blot out his mother's pleading look.

Then he heard a voice behind him, cold and level in the darkening air.

"She's going to die."

Jason turned, and there was an old, wizened man with a fishing rod and a tin pail standing over him.

His shadow lay long on the sand.

The man spoke again, pointing with a long, bony finger at the newspaper.

"She's guilty, and she's going to get what's coming to her."

"And that's what you want," Jason said.

"That what I want. That's what the whole town wants. There's not a single person I know who thinks differently," the man said.

"Not a single one."

"No."

Jason looked up at the cruel, thin lips. "Do you believe in God?" he asked suddenly.

His voice was icy and quiet.

His gray eyes piercing.

The man stared at him.

"What?"

"Well, do you?" Jason asked.

"Of course I do. Been going to church all my life."

"And praying?"

The man nodded. "And praying. What are you driving at?"

"Just this."

"Just what?"

Jason shook his head grimly. "Just that it's done you no good. No good at all."

"What do you mean?" the man asked.

"You could just as well have been going to a movie house."

"Movie . . . ?"

"That's right. Watching John Wayne and Clint Eastwood riding their horses into the sunset," Jason said.

"I don't get you. Don't get you at all."

"I know you don't."

Jason got up and looked bitterly at the man. "No use talking to you. To you or the rest of the world. No use at all."

He walked away from the man and into the approaching darkness.

"Hey, wait. Wait a second," the man called out.

Jason stopped and turned.

The old man came up to him.

"Well?" Jason asked grimly.

"Why did you say that to me?" There was a hurt and bewildered look in the old eyes.

"Why?"

You were talking about my mother, Jason wanted to shout at him. You want to see my mother dead.

You and that whole town of yours.

You're all nothing but bloodthirsty savages.

All of you.

Mindless, heartless beasts.

The man came closer to him and raised his fishing rod high as if it were a staff.

"Sure I believe in God," he said. "A just God. What's wrong in that?"

"Nothing."

"Then what are you talking about?"

"I used to believe in a merciful God," Jason said.

And he walked away from the startled old man.

Chapter

28

Have I truly lost faith?

Have I?

Or am I crying out against the savagery and cruelty of people?

Is it that?

If my mother is saved, will I regain my belief?

Will I?

Will I honestly believe again?

Honestly?

For it has to be honest.

It must be that or nothing at all.

And if . . . if she dies?

What then?

Dear God, what then?

Chapter

29

The night was in his favor. It was dark, starless, with only a bright sliver of moon in the black sky. As he neared Thornton, he saw that a street fair was being held in the center of town.

He changed his plan.

Instead of going through the city, he drove around it until he found the road that led to one of the bays that emptied into the Gulf.

Jason drove along the road until he came to Crawford Lane.

A sad, pensive look came into his eyes when he saw the road sign. He used to have a close friend who lived on Crawford Lane.

Tom Wilson.

They were in class together.

Jason wondered now what had happened to him and if he still lived there.

Tom's father was a teacher in the Thornton school system.

Jason slowed the car down when he came to the house. He read the name, and then he sped away into the darkness.

They're still there.

What does Tom think about Marian Feldon?

And Mr. Wilson? How does he feel about her?

Do they want her to die?

Tom had a good and warm heart, and my mother was decent to him all the time.

Is his heart now as hard and cruel as all the rest?

Why shouldn't it be?

And his father?

What about him?

My mother saved his job for him one time.

I remember how he almost wept when he came to thank her.

I'll bet he's forgotten that now.

I'll bet my life on that.

He's like the rest of them.

Put her to death.

To death.

I can hear his voice.

I can hear all their voices.

Self-righteous hypocrites.

They talk of law and order and civilized living, but in their hearts, their secret hearts, they cry out for murder.

They long to kill.

They do.

She's guilty.

The court says she's guilty.

So kill her.

Kill her.

"Kill her!" Jason shouted.

His hands gripped the wheel and jerked it to one side. The car swerved off the road and headed for a tree.

He jammed his foot on the brake just in time.

Jason sat back and put his hand over his eyes.

I must control myself.

I must.

Or I'll blow it all.
He stared through the windshield at the night and sighed.
I've got a job to do, he said grimly to himself.
And I'd better do it.
Or she'll die.

Chapter
30

He drove down the bleak tree-lined lane and he thought.
   If she dies, what will happen to me?
   How will I go through life carrying her death?
   I couldn't.
   I know I couldn't.
   I'll be destroyed along with her.
   In killing her, they will also be killing me.

Chapter

31

The lane turned and began to follow the gray edge of the bay.
There were flat stretches of dark, silver-tipped uncut grass
that lay between lone houses and level, rippling water. A few
of the houses were lit, but the rest were dark and empty
looking. Each one had a long wooden dock and, at its end,
a gray boat, dim and thinly gleaming, moored and swaying
in the night current.

He drove along about a half mile, the tires of his car making the only sound, and then he saw ahead the wavering
outline of Morgan's house.

It stood, two stories high, black and silent.

Its windows, unshaded, glimmering in the pale moonlight.

"There it is," he whispered.

Jason slowed the car down and looked about him. He saw
nothing but the dark reach of water on one side and wide,
stark fields on the other.

Isolation.

Complete, soundless isolation.

Morgan had wanted to be by himself, Jason thought
grimly. Nobody around. He used to live in the center of

Thornton, just a short block from police headquarters, but after his wife and children walked away from him, he moved out and became a loner.

Where there's nothing but water and grass and a lonely road.

He lived alone, and now he's dying alone.

Staring into the fires of hell.

His soul hanging in the balance.

All depends on whether I succeed or fail.

All depends on that.

Jason drove past the silent house until he came to an empty field.

"This will do it," he murmured.

Then he drove the car onto the grass and stopped it under the cover of an old and heavy-branched tree.

The black Honda blended with the darkness of the night.

It would be hard to see the car from the road, he said to himself.

A perfect cover.

Jason reached over and took a small flashlight from the glove compartment and put it into his jacket pocket. Then he got out of the car and quietly, carefully, closed the door.

Yet the click of the door latch seemed loud and threatening to him.

He breathed out low and then stood in the darkness and thought.

I must get in and out of the house as quickly as I can.

Find the documents, look over them, and then beat it back to the car and head for Lauderdale.

Jason felt in his pocket for the keys. They were cold to his fingers. Then he began to walk along the deserted road toward the house. His footsteps had a hollow echo.

From far out on the water, the sound of a boat whistle, faint and sad, floated in to him. He paused and listened to it. And then he went on.

As he neared the house, the tension built up within him.

I'm alone, he said to himself.

There's no one around.

93

No one knows I'm here.

I'm alone, and it will be all right.

It will.

It has to.

Suddenly the headlights of an approaching car cut through the darkness and startled him.

The lights came nearer and grew larger.

Jason looked desperately about him, saw a tree, and slid behind its shelter. He stood there, his breath short, until the car passed and sped on into the night, its taillights glowing like two red signals of danger.

He watched them melt away into the darkness.

All became still and soundless again.

Jason turned and walked on.

The only sound he now heard was that of his footsteps on the macadam.

One after another.

Then the sound suddenly stopped.

He found himself standing in front of the wooden house and looking up at the silent windows.

My mother's life is in this house, he said to himself.

He looked away and out over the glimmering water of the bay.

Far in the distance he could see the wavering lights of the slowly moving fishing boats, shining like low, flickering stars.

For an instant he thought of the Esplanade and of Carla sitting at his side, her warm, comforting body close to his.

Then he turned away from the tiny points of light and back to the shadowy outlines of the house.

His lips thinned into a hard line.

He clenched his hands tight and walked up the wooden steps and onto the dark porch.

Jason looked about him warily and then went to the door and took out the keys.

Just as he was about to put the key into one of the locks, he stopped and froze.

There at the end of the porch, at waist-high level, were two eyes staring at him.

Staring and glowing.

Then the eyes moved slowly away from him, and he heard the soft sound of a small body landing on its feet and then the gliding movement of the cat as it slid past him and down the steps into the night.

Jason put his hand to his forehead and drew it away wet.

I'm scared to my guts, he said to himself.

Scared.

And I'm going to be scared all the way.

But I'll live with it.

I've got to.

He opened the door and stepped inside the house. Then he slowly, quietly, closed the door behind him.

He stood flat against it, his senses sharp and alert.

Listening.

Listening.

He heard nothing but the silence of emptiness.

Jason snapped on the flashlight and let its beam course over the living room.

The furniture stood there, motionless and abandoned.

A glass on an end table gleamed.

Jason felt a desolated sadness as he looked about the room, and he thought of Morgan sitting in one of the chairs.

Alone.

So desperately alone.

And then he thought of his mother sitting alone in her cell.

Her eyes dark and fathomless.

Waiting for her death.

He turned away from the shadowy chair and walked down a narrow hallway and into the small kitchen.

He stopped and listened to the sound of water as it leaked from a faucet in steady drops onto the hard metallic surface of the sink.

It rasped his nerves.

Jason went over to the faucet and turned it hard, but the dripping went on relentlessly.

He left the kitchen and went to the staircase that led to the upstairs rooms.

Jason guided the beam over the dusty steps and began ascending.

Slow step by step.

He stopped stock-still when he heard the motor of a car coming close to the house, and his hand gripped the banister tight until he could hear the car moving away down the road.

Finally, the silence of the night blotted out the sound.

All was still again.

He reached the top of the stairs and then let his flashlight play over the gray walls and bare ceiling and then into the open doorways of the bedrooms.

Jason went into the largest bedroom, stood silent for an instant, and then walked to the closet and opened the door.

"Yes," he whispered.

Morgan's clothes hung in a dark row before him.

Jason pushed aside some of the suits and let the beam go over the wall.

The wall had cedar panels from ceiling to floor.

Jason searched along the panels until he found a tiny pencil mark.

No larger than a dot.

From there he measured off six inches, using the knuckle of his thumb as a ruler.

With the moist palm of his hand he pressed hard on the spot and was gripped by panic when nothing happened.

The panel would not move.

"No," he said and again, "No."

He bit his lip, and then he stepped back and measured again.

This time the spot was just a bit more to the right.

A half inch at most.

He pressed hard again, and then he felt one of the panels begin to slide toward the right wall.

He sighed. Now he saw the outlines of the small safe and the gleam of a knob.

He had memorized the combination, and now he turned

the knob first to the left and then all around again and then to the right and then a few notches to the right again, and he stopped.

He took his hand away from the knob, closed his eyes, and prayed silently.

Then he opened his eyes again, put his hand to the knob, and turned.

The door opened.

"Yes," he whispered.

His voice sounded loud, and it startled him.

He stood rigid and listened.

He heard nothing but his own heavy breathing.

Jason put his hand into the safe and felt along until he found the folder and he drew it out.

He went over to the white-sheeted bed and sat down on it.

Then he opened the folder and drew out the top page and began reading it under the beam of the flashlight.

"I, Captain Frank Morgan, of the Thornton Police Department, do hereby swear that all that is stated here is true. I find that what I testified to in court was completely false. My testimony was completely at variance with the facts. I was gravely misled by my prejudices and arrogance, as were the other police officers who were assigned to the case.

"The evidence I have slowly and painstakingly gathered here will prove beyond any doubt that Marian Feldon is absolutely innocent of the crime of murder. . . ."

Jason bowed his head silently.

Finally, he stirred himself and glanced quickly at the other documents.

He came upon two names mentioned again and again.

Albert White.

George Fuller.

"It's all here," he whispered. "All of it."

He put the documents back into the folder.

He hurried over to the closet, closed the safe, and slid the panel back into place again.

He stood looking at the blank wall.

No one would ever suspect that there was a safe behind it, he said to himself.

Morgan's a good detective.

He knows how to hide things.

And how to find them.

Jason pushed the suits together again and softly shut the closet door.

He leaned against it to catch his breath, the folder tight in his hands.

He still gripped it as he walked down the shadowy stairs.

When he came to the front door, he stopped.

He listened to the dripping faucet in the kitchen.

Slow drop after slow drop.

Onto the hard metallic surface of the sink.

That was the last sound he heard when he closed the door of the house and stepped again into the night.

Chapter

32

He felt that someone was watching him.

As he walked along the road, he turned a few times, but there was no one there.

Only black silence.

He walked again, his footsteps sounding sharp and lone against the stillness that lay about him.

The folder was gripped in his hand.

And he thought of Morgan lying on his bed, waiting for him.

Of his mother standing by the cell window and looking out into the dread night.

Waiting for him.

Somehow she knew what he was doing.

She must know.

She must.

He came to the field and walked along it, treading the whispering grass underfoot, and soon he was under the cover of the huge tree.

She must know, he said to himself.

She's waiting.

Chapter

33

He opened the trunk of the car and then lifted up the carpet that lay there and put the folder far under it. Then he set the carpet back into place and carefully scanned it.

His eyes went over every inch.

No one could tell that the carpet had been moved.

Or even touched.

Perfect.

That's exactly where Morgan would have hidden the folder, Jason said to himself.

I'm sure of it.

From now on I've got to sit in his skull.

Think and act the way he would.

And I'll be able to get the documents back to him.

I will.

Jason closed the trunk and got into the car.

He sat for a moment and stared through the windshield and down the length of the field and out over the water.

Out.

Far out where the lights of the fishing boats were.

Still flickering.

Like tiny stars.

He turned away from them, and it was then that he saw the two glowing eyes low in the field.

Fixed upon him.

The eyes of the cat.

Jason gazed into them and shivered.

Then the eyes swung away and disappeared into the dark.

Yet he still saw them.

Glowing fiercely at him.

Jason drove the black Honda from under the cover of the tree, across the dark field, and back onto the road.

It was only then that he turned on the headlights.

The beam cut through the night like a naked blade.

The road stretched bare and silent before him.

Chapter

34

Two names.

Albert White.

George Fuller.

Two names.

Of two murderers.

One Morgan claimed had ordered the killing, and the other had actually done it.

Albert White.

George Fuller.

Two names.

Jason listened to the hypnotic sound of the tires going over the road, and all he heard were two names.

Albert White.

George Fuller.

His hatred for the two men surged within him, and he found it hard to breathe.

He had to pull over to the side of the road and stop the car.

They killed, and now others would kill my mother.

An innocent woman.

They would sit back and let her die for their crime.

Frame her and then sit back and smile.

Smile while the executioner pulled the switch and her body shivered with the bolts of electricity smashing through it.

Smile.

He clenched his hands tight and cried out in a low, tortured voice:

"Mother."

And then he was silent.

A gray van went past him and disappeared into the night.

Jason stirred himself, started the car again, and turned it back onto the road.

He increased the speed.

But the sound would not leave him.

Would give him no peace.

Albert White.

George Fuller.

Two names.

Of two murderers.

Murderers.

Chapter

35

He drove down the dark, deserted road, and just where it turned away from the bay, he jammed on the brakes and came to an abrupt stop.

A chill went through him.

There ahead of him, blocking the road, was the gray van.

And then he saw a figure get out of the van and come slowly toward him.

As it came closer into the glare of the headlights, he recognized the man.

The lean, hard face and the cold eyes.

The flat voice.

"Hello, kid."

It was Ed Carter.

"Mind if I get a hitch with you?"

He opened the door and got into the car and sat down next to Jason.

"Thanks."

"What do you want?" Jason asked.

"Just a ride. You owe me one."

"What?"

"A short one," the man said.

And now Jason saw the gun pointed at his head.

"Okay, kid?"

"What's this all about?"

"Nothing. See that van?" Carter said.

And Jason saw the van back up and then turn and head down the road toward Thornton.

"Follow it," Carter ordered.

Now the gun barrel was in his side.

"Faster."

Jason drove behind the van, his face white and taut.

"What do you want from me?" Jason asked.

"Just drive and shut up."

"You've got the wrong person. You're making a mistake."

Carter shook his head grimly. "No mistake."

"But I tell you that I—"

"Drive," Carter cut in harshly. "And no tricks. Or you die."

And then he added quietly, "And nobody will ever find you again."

Chapter

36

He followed the van through the crowded streets of Thornton, past the bright, festive lights and the holiday noise of the fair, a bleak feeling within him, bleak and lost, and then he had to stop for a red light

The van ahead of him.

Always ahead of him.

Like a cruel, heartless fate.

Jason looked to his side desperately, and then he felt a sudden warm thrill sweep through him.

For there, parked at the curb, was a police car.

The policeman's face was turned to him.

The cool eyes appraising Jason.

And it was at that instant that Jason was about to cry out to him for help when he felt the gun barrel jammed hard into his side and he heard Carter's flat voice.

"Don't try it. Or you'll be dead before your mother gets hers."

Jason's lips closed shut.

The policeman turned his eyes away from him.

The light changed, the van moved on, and Jason followed it, feeling all hope drain away from him.

I'm losing, he said to himself.

Losing it all.

I can see that now.

See it so clearly.

She was doomed.

Doomed from the very beginning.

There is no mercy in this world.

There is no justice.

None.

None.

There is nothing but savagery and death.

Death.

Sing me a death song, Jason.

Sing, my son.

Let your voice be the last one I hear.

The last.

Chapter
37

He followed the van out of Thornton and onto the coast high-way that runs alongside the white shadowy beaches down to Naples.

He passed pale stucco houses that gleamed in the night and high-rise hotels with brightly lit windows and softly glowing terraces.

He felt he could hear the low voices of the guests as they strolled about the grounds after a late dinner.

Voices of casually dressed people content with life and the serene world around them.

Content and secure, he thought bitterly.

The hotels disappeared into the night, and for a long stretch he saw dark water with low white-capped waves rolling in to shore, and he felt a sore longing to be out on the Gulf once more, only once more, as he used to do with his mother, but now with Carla, just with Carla at his side.

The two of them silent.

With not a single word to each other.

Just to be out there under the vast, endless night and never to come in to shore again.

Never.

He looked away from the reach of water and back to the long, lonely highway.

"Never," he whispered.

His voice was lost in the night.

Never.

The car sped on behind the gray van.

As if it had been linked to it with an unbreakable chain.

Mile after relentless mile.

And now he thought of Lydia waiting for him to return, standing on the terrace, her figure dark against the morning sky, watching him leave.

Her face tight and mournful.

Her eyes full of sorrow.

Bleak with the same despair that was ever in his mother's eyes.

As if she were foreseeing his fate.

It's no use, Jason.

Don't go.

Don't leave me.

You're going to fail.

You're going to die.

Jason, my Jason.

Come back to me.

Come back, my son.

I'm your mother now, Jason.

Your mother.

"Lydia," he whispered.

He stared through the windshield and drove on.

And all the time, Carter sat silently at Jason's side, like a shadow, the gun in his lean hand.

Jason looked down and saw the harsh glint of the barrel.

You live by that gun, he thought bitterly.

And someday you'll die by that gun.

But I won't see that day.

I'm sure now that I won't.

He drove on.

Chapter

38

"We're going to make a turn soon," Carter said.

Jason didn't speak.

"Didn't you hear me?"

"Yes."

Carter looked at him. "Just take it easy, kid. Don't look so sad."

"Sure," Jason said.

"You've got guts. I like that."

Jason was silent.

"Some other kid would be scared out of his skull. Crying. Begging for mercy. But you sit there with a poker face. I like that."

"And I hate your guts," Jason said.

Carter laughed low. "And if I handed over this gun to you, you'd kill me, wouldn't you?"

Jason shook his head grimly. "I don't believe in killing."

"But you'd hold the gun on me," Carter said.

"I'd hold the gun."

"And put a bullet in my shoulder to make me behave."

"I'd do that," Jason said.

110

Carter laughed. "You're okay. Listen to me. You cooperate and you'll be all right."

"What do you mean?" Jason asked.

"You do what we want and you'll go home alive."

"And what do you want me to do?"

"You'll find out."

"Why don't you tell me now?" Jason asked.

Carter shook his head and pointed to the van. "Just follow. It's making the turn now."

The van swung off the highway and into a shadowy, winding lane. Jason drove along behind the now slow-moving van. He saw no houses, only clusters of tall trees, dark, with large, heavy leaves. And beyond the wall of leaves a touch of wavering moonlight. The touch of light made the lane seem even darker.

I feel as if I'm leaving my life behind me, he thought.

Leaving it forever.

As if I never lived it.

Never had a mother.

Or met Carla.

Lived with Lydia.

All, all is being smothered by this darkness.

Suddenly the lane came to an end at a curving driveway. Jason saw a large, sprawling house loom before him. It was of white brick, and it stood overlooking the faintly gleaming water of the Gulf.

The house had a wide front picture window.

Its white blinds were drawn shut.

Jason followed the van into the driveway, up to the silent house, and then stopped the car.

"We're here," Carter said.

Then Jason saw the driver of the van get out and come slowly over to them.

"All set?" he asked.

He was a short, stocky man with a diamond ring on his stubby middle finger.

The ring glittered in the night.

A cold glitter.

111

"Yes, Al," Carter said.

The man's hostile brown eyes scanned Jason's face.

"Give you any trouble?"

His voice was low and harsh.

Carter shook his head. "The kid's okay."

"He's not okay. Get him in to see George."

"Sure."

Carter turned to Jason. "The man's waiting for you inside. Let's go."

Jason got out of the car and stepped onto the hard pavement of the driveway. For an instant he felt his knees start to give, and then he clenched his hands tight and straightened up. His eyes were fierce.

The two men watched him with impassive faces.

"Come on," Carter said, his gun on Jason.

They walked through the still night to the front door of the house.

No one spoke.

Carter knocked softly on the wooden door.

Three times.

They waited.

Then someone opened the door without a word, and they went into the house.

The heavy door closed shut behind Jason.

I'll never come out of this house alive, Jason said to himself.

Never.

Chapter

39

And with my death my mother dies, too.
   My mother, of the bleak, sad eyes.
   And silent lips.
   Yet I hear her.
   Ever hear her.
   Sing me a death song, Jason.
   Sing me a death song, my son.
   Let it be the last words I hear.
   The last.

Chapter

40

A death song.

"Just relax. No one is going to harm you." The man's voice was soft and pleasant.

Jason looked silently at him.

"I assure you. No one," the man continued.

He was as tall as Jason and had a lithe and easy-moving body. He wore a white silk shirt, open at the neck, tan slacks, and brown alligator-skin shoes.

His face was lean and tan.

His hair was dark and smooth, with narrow streaks of gray.

He wore rimless glasses over gentle blue eyes.

The lips were thin and bloodless.

They were all standing in a brightly lit living room that had white glistening leather furniture.

There were several pieces of bronze sculpture on the various end tables.

One, Jason recognized as a small, exquisite Noguchi.

He had seen its mate in one of the New York galleries.

Lydia had been there with him and admired it.

"I'd buy it, Jason. But it's a bit too expensive for me," she had said.

Lydia, and her world, now seemed so far, far away.

On the coffee table in the center of the huge room were two large art books. One of Gaugin's paintings and the other of Jasper Johns'.

I'm in the home of a cultivated man, Jason thought grimly.

A cultivated killer.

And they are the worst of all killers.

The man put out a delicate but firm hand to Jason.

"I'm George Fuller. And you are Jason Feldon."

"He's called Ross up in New York," Carter said.

"I know," Fuller said quietly, noting that Jason did not take his hand.

"He lives with Lydia Ross. She's his mother now to everybody up there."

"I know that, too," Fuller said.

Then he turned back to Jason and motioned to one of the leather chairs.

"Sit down, Jason."

Jason didn't move.

"The man told you to sit," Al said harshly. He gripped Jason's arm.

"Take your hand off him," Fuller said sharply.

Al paled and moved quickly away from Jason. "Sure, George."

"Get out of here. The two of you," Fuller ordered.

The two silently left the room, and Jason was now alone with Fuller.

"I must apologize for them. They're nothing but animals."

"But necessary ones," Jason said.

Fuller looked at Jason and smiled. "You understand this imperfect world, don't you?"

And then he said, still studying Jason, "But you've had

to. Or you would have ended up in an asylum. Isn't that so, Jason?''

Jason didn't answer.

"It is so. You've rid yourself of all illusions.''

"I have,'' Jason said.

"There are none left, are there?''

"None.''

"Yes. It's there in your face. In your attitude. It's there,'' Fuller said. He nodded and came closer to Jason.

"Did the animals hurt you in any way?'' he asked.

"No.''

"Were they rough with you?''

Jason shook his head.

"Good. I gave them strict orders to handle you gently. Just to bring you here to me. Just that.''

"And if I didn't want to come?'' Jason asked.

Fuller smiled. "But you did come, didn't you?''

"With a gun at my head,'' Jason said.

"True,'' Fuller said softly. "Quite true.''

He patted Jason on the shoulder and saw him flinch. "Easy, Jason.''

He pointed to two long glass doors that opened onto a large stone terrace. The terrace overlooked the dark, softly gleaming waters of the Gulf.

"Why don't you come out there with me? You can sit in the pleasant night air and begin to relax.'' Fuller made a step to the doors, but Jason didn't move.

"Tell me,'' Jason said.

Fuller paused and turned to him.

"Yes?''

"What do you want of me?'' Jason asked in an intense voice. "What?''

But Fuller didn't answer him. "Just come out there with me. Let me help you rid yourself of your fears. You do have them, don't you?''

"I'm all right,'' Jason said.

Fuller shook his head. "You're brave. You're admirable.

116

But very frightened. And you should be, under the circumstances. You should be, Jason." He moved quietly and decisively over to Jason. "So come out there with me."

Fuller took Jason by the arm and led him out of the brightly lit room and onto the terrace. He motioned to a wicker chair and then watched Jason slowly sink down upon its cushion.

"That's better," he murmured.

Fuller went over to a black iron scroll railing and leaned against it, casually and easily.

He held up a pack of cigarettes.

"Do you smoke?"

"No," Jason said.

"Care for a drink? Calm you down a bit."

"No."

"There is nothing you want?"

"Nothing."

"Now what do I want? Just to talk to you. That's all," Fuller said. His shadow lay long and angular on the flagstones of the terrace. "I want to clear your mind of some misconceptions."

"What do you mean?" Jason asked.

"Of lies."

Jason looked past the dark figure and out to the glimmering water and waited.

Far out into the night he could see the pale shadow of a sail, and he watched it move slowly, ever so slowly, like a ghost, until it was lost.

Then he heard the man's low and persuasive voice. "You've been fed a lot of lies. Lies by a man who is truly out of his mind. Believe me, Jason."

Fuller paused again.

The lenses of his rimless glasses gleamed in the darkness.

"I know all that Frank Morgan has told you."

"I don't know any Frank Morgan," Jason said.

"Of course you don't."

Fuller was silent.

And then he spoke again.

"You've heard nothing but the ravings of a man who is crazed by his fear of death and what comes after it. His mind has been destroyed by his illness."

"I don't know what you're talking about."

"It's a cancerous mind, Jason."

Fuller took out a white cigarette and lit it. "It's like a sieve. Eaten through. It can no longer hold any sense of reality or of logic."

The match flared into the darkness and then died.

Now only the glow of the cigarette remained.

A little stab of red.

"I tell you I don't know any Frank Morgan," Jason said.

"Then what were you doing in his house?"

"I don't even know where his house is."

"What were you looking for?"

Jason didn't answer.

The acrid smoke of the cigarette drifted over to him.

"Did you find any papers?"

"No," Jason said.

Fuller laughed low, and his even white teeth gleamed in the darkness.

"We didn't, either. We've been through that house from top to bottom, and there is nothing. Absolutely nothing."

He laughed low again.

"Morgan had me believing in those imaginary documents. Even me. I heard about them and decided to investigate. Nothing, Jason. Nothing. There are none. Never were any. Believe what I say to you."

His voice became cold and hard. "He sent you on a mad errand."

Jason was silent.

"Mad and potentially deadly. Do you hear me?" Fuller said.

Jason slowly nodded.

"Do you want to know why?" Fuller continued.

"Yes."

"Because the man hates your mother and hates the son of

118

that mother. You didn't see him in court as I did. You didn't see him in the years after. His hatred poured out of his sick body. He became paranoid. He can't wait to see her die. And to torture you with false hopes.''

Jason watched the figure abruptly turn and toss the white cigarette over the railing into the water below.

"Torture you.''

There was silence.

Then he heard Fuller speak again. This time his voice was low and gentle. "Jason, listen to me. Please.''

A shred of moonlight fell upon his dark hair and silvered it.

The rimless glasses flashed as he spoke.

"Your mother is going to be executed. There is nothing anyone can do about it.''

"Nothing,'' Jason whispered.

"Jason, you're a realist. You must accept that fact. Horrible and unacceptable as it is. You must do it. Or you'll go the way Frank Morgan did. Your mind will give out on you. And you'll be living in a fantasy world.''

He paused and spoke again.

"Facts, Jason. Not insane lies. I had nothing to do with Arthur Madison's death. Nothing. They claim that your mother killed him. I don't know. But I do know that I did not.''

"Morgan says that you owed him money,'' Jason said.

"Morgan. Yes, it's true. But why should I kill a man who owed me money? Is there any logic to that? Isn't it more logical and sane to wait until he is able to repay that debt. Isn't it, Jason?''

Jason didn't speak.

"Well?''

"What do you want of me?'' Jason said.

"Just this. That you forget the lies that Morgan told you. That you rid yourself of them. Once and for all.''

"Why?''

"Because lies are always dangerous. One never knows where they lead to. One never knows, Jason.''

119

"And if I rid myself of the lies?" Jason asked.

"You are free to go."

Jason was silent.

"You'll spend the night here, and in the morning you can leave," Fuller said.

"I can drive away?"

"Yes."

Jason stared through the night at the man, the dark, almost obscure figure.

He could not see the eyes behind the rimless glasses.

Yet he thought he could make out the trace of a smile on the lips of the man.

The thin lips.

Then he heard the soft, persuasive voice.

"Well, Jason?"

Was it a mocking smile?

Cruel and mocking?

"How do you know I won't be lying to you?" Jason said.

"I will know."

"Yes. I guess you will."

"I've been around a long time, Jason. In a very dangerous business. Many people have tried to fool me. But very few have succeeded."

And paid with their lives when they did succeed, Jason thought.

Now he was sure the smile was gone from the thin lips.

"Well, Jason?"

The voice was now cold and commanding.

"I believe you."

"And you do see the truth?"

"Yes," Jason said.

"Not the distortion that Morgan has done to it. Not that."

"I can see that now."

Fuller came away from the railing and stood over Jason.

"I believe you, Jason," he said quietly.

You don't believe me, Jason thought.

And I don't believe you.

We are both liars.

"Come inside and we'll have some coffee," Fuller said.
Jason rose and followed him in.
I'll never leave this house alive, he said to himself.
Never.

Chapter

41

He was sitting at the table, watching silently as Fuller had his coffee, when a dark-haired, middle-aged woman came quietly into the room.

She paused and looked at him.

Fuller rose.

"Donna. I thought you were sleeping."

She wore a pink robe, and her face was pale.

She had dark, sad eyes.

Her voice was low and gentle.

"I was, George. But then I heard you speaking on the terrace."

"I'm sorry if I woke you."

"It's no matter. I don't sleep much these days."

"You don't," Fuller said softly.

He put his arm around her, and Jason thought he saw her flinch, ever so slightly, and then he wasn't sure of it.

Fuller turned to Jason.

"Donna, this is Jason Ross. Jason, my wife."

She smiled at Jason and then sat down at the table, just across from him.

Fuller stood over them.

"Shall I get you some coffee?"

"Yes, George," she said.

"You, Jason?"

"No, thanks."

"Had enough."

"Yes," Jason said.

Fuller went over to the range and turned on a jet.

"Jason is the son of a business friend of mine."

"Oh," Donna said.

The dark eyes were gently studying Jason.

"He comes from New York. Been visiting some relatives in Fort Myers."

"You're staying the night?" Donna asked.

"Yes," Jason said.

"He's leaving the first thing in the morning," Fuller said.

"That's too bad," Donna said, looking at Jason. "Why can't you stay awhile with us? Wouldn't you like to?"

Jason didn't answer.

"We have a very large pool. Beautiful tennis courts. You do play tennis, don't you?" she said.

"A bit," Jason said.

"I'm sure you made your school team. Didn't you?"

Jason silently nodded.

"I play a fair game. I'll give you some competition," she said.

"Donna," Fuller said. "He has to get back home."

But she didn't seem to hear him.

"I'm alone most of the time. George is always away somewhere. We'll be pleasant company for each other, Jason."

"He has to go," Fuller said.

Donna was silent.

And then she murmured, "It's a shame."

Jason looked away from her to Fuller, standing silent and tall at the other end of the room.

Then he heard her soft voice.

"Where do you live in New York, Jason?"

123

"Manhattan."

"Where in Manhattan?" she asked.

"On the East Side."

"Near Madison Avenue?"

"Yes," he said.

She laughed a soft, pleased laugh. There was now a trace of color in the pale face. "I go up three times a year to do my shopping there. There are no stores in the world like the Madison Avenue shops. Isn't that so, George?"

"It's so."

"But they're very expensive, aren't they?" And she laughed again.

"They are," Fuller said. He came over to the table with her cup and then sat down.

"Thanks, George." She patted him on the arm, and Jason noticed with a shock that two of her middle fingers were missing.

She saw him looking at the mutilated hand, and for an instant her eyes became cold and her face taut and hard, and then the instant vanished.

Her low voice was animated when she spoke again. "There's one boutique on Sixty-second street that I've been going to for many years, Jason. It's such a delight to walk into it and see again the familiar faces. A delight, Jason."

She sat there sipping her coffee and talking about the shops and the clothes and the plays she went to, and all the time he felt that she was studying him.

Even after she got up and said good night to them and left the room, he felt her presence still there with him.

Jason heard Fuller's quiet and impassive voice break into his thoughts.

"It's time to go to bed."

Jason nodded.

Fuller walked with him to a bedroom and then paused on the threshold.

"You have everything you'll need."

"Yes."

"I'll see you in the morning."

The hall light flashed from the rimless glasses.
"Sleep well," Fuller said.
Then the door closed shut.
And Jason was alone again.

Chapter

42

He lay, fully clothed, hour after long hour, staring up at the dim white ceiling.

He heard a clock chime three times.

He listened.

And then the silence crept back into the large house again.

He lay there, tense and restless.

Finally, his eyes closed from sheer exhaustion.

He slept.

He dreamed of his mother standing over him, her eyes bleak with sorrow.

Sorrow and final despair.

It's over, Jason.

You've failed, dear son.

I know how hard you've tried.

And I know that you are about to lose your own life.

I know it, dear son.

But of what use was it all?

He's won.

That evil being has won.

There is no justice in this world, Jason.

There never was.

None, my son.

None.

"Jason."

He heard her sad voice again.

"Jason."

He opened his eyes, and Donna was standing over him.

She put her finger to his lips.

Her face was taut and cold.

"Don't speak," she whispered. "Just listen."

He sat up in bed and stared through the half darkness at her grim form.

"You're not leaving here in the morning. He'll make up an excuse and keep you until your mother is executed. And then he'll have you killed and your body dumped in the Gulf."

A thin ray of moonlight was on her face.

Her sad eyes gleamed.

"Your car is now parked deep in the lane. No one will hear you drive away from that spot. Get on the highway and go up to Tampa. You'll find a plane from there to New York."

"Tampa?" he whispered.

She nodded.

"Not Lauderdale. Eagan is waiting for you there. He's sold out to Fuller. That's how Fuller knew every move you were making."

Then he heard her voice again.

"The two hoods are sleeping. Fuller is sleeping. So get out of here. Now."

"What will happen to you?"

She held up her mutilated hand.

"He did this. He'll do worse this time."

Jason stood up, looking at her through the darkness.

He thought he could see tears glistening in her eyes.

Then he heard her voice, and now it was soft and heart-rending to him. "You're like the son I never had. So it will be worth it."

127

He stood there, hesitant to go.

She came close to him.

"Go, Jason. Go. And then forget me. I've lived with him. I'm just as bad as he is for staying with him. Go. And forget me."

He turned away from her and went out of the room.

As long as he lived, he never forgot her.

Chapter

43

And he never forgot the moment he stood in the hospital room, with Walter Todman at his side, watching Morgan as he signed one document after another. And then the notary putting his seal on each one.

Morgan sighed and then leaned back onto his pillow.

"I've spoken to the governor," Todman said.

Morgan's eyes were closed.

But his lips moved.

He spoke in a frail voice.

"She'll be free now."

"Yes," Todman said.

"I'll die a better death."

The notary left, and then Todman left with the papers to catch a plane to Florida.

Jason was now alone with the dying man.

"Jason?" he said. "Come closer. I can hardly hear you."

Jason approached the bed and stood silent.

Morgan opened his eyes and looked up at him.

"Your aunt Lydia."

Jason waited.

"They loved the same man. That's why Lydia went to live in New York. The two sisters loved the same man."

He paused and then spoke again.

"I just wanted you to know that."

"Yes," Jason whispered.

Morgan lay there a long time without a word, his eyes resting on Jason's face.

He slowly raised his thin, wrinkled hand.

The hand of an old man.

"Jason," he whispered.

Jason leaned closer to hear him.

"Yes?"

"Do you think your mother will forgive me?"

Jason tried to speak but couldn't.

"Do you think you could get her to come here and—"

"I'll bring her," Jason finally said.

Morgan's old eyes brightened.

"You will?"

"Yes," Jason said.

"Promise?"

"I promise."

Morgan's eyes closed again.

He died that night.

Chapter

44

He stood with Lydia and Walter Todman in the Florida sun, waiting.

And then the moment came.

He saw her come out of the building and stand on the stone steps.

"Go to her, Jason," Lydia said.

He tried to move but still stood rooted to the spot.

"Jason."

He heard the voice come through the shining air to him.

And then he found himself running.

"Jason," she said.

He held her tight.

And it was only then that the tears came.

About the Author

Jay Bennett, a master of suspense, was the first writer to win in two successive years the Mystery Writers of America's prestigious Edgar Allan Poe Award for Best Juvenile Mystery. His book *The Skeleton Man* was nominated for the 1986 Edgar Allan Poe Award. He is the author of many suspense novels for young adults as well as successful adult novels, stage plays, and television scripts. Mr. Bennett lives in Cherry Hill, New Jersey.